LEONIE
GANT

CURSE

THE

DARK

The Harstone Legacy
Book I

ISBN-13: 978-0-9943999-3-9

To Mike, Samuel and Nicholas.
I don't know what I did to deserve you, but it must have been
something good.

"*S*on of a..." I gripped my pounding head and curled into the fetal position, trying to breathe through the pain while cursing my decision to sit up in what I could now see was an enclosed space.

It took several moments for my brain to dislodge the fogginess of sleep and the reality of my position became evident to me. As I processed my surroundings, several things hit me at once. Despite my first impressions, the darkness around me was broken by extremely thin slivers of light, and I could hear and feel the rumbling of an engine. I was also being thrown around within the small space I had found myself in. I was in the trunk of a car and, even though I had no memory of how I had ended up here, I knew without a shadow of a doubt that I hadn't got in here willingly. My stomach churned as a number of chilling scenarios careened through my head, but I kept coming back to the most obvious. I had been kidnapped. I didn't know who and I didn't know why, but there was one thing I knew with absolute certainty. They had the wrong person, and when they realized their mistake, I was going to be in a lot of trouble. Or at least, a lot more trouble than I was in right at this moment.

There was nothing in my life that justified me being kidnapped. I was a librarian, not usually considered a high-risk occupation. I wasn't walking down a dark alleyway. I hadn't accidentally witnessed a mob boss killing one of his underlings. I didn't have an ex-boyfriend who would give me a passing thought, let alone feel the need to stalk me. In essence, I was the last person in the world who should be kidnapped. And yet, it seemed I had been. I tried to concentrate in an effort to work out what had happened. The last thing I remember was opening my front door to what I assumed was my regular pizza guy, Chet, who constituted the closest relationship I had these days. Instead, I found a woman old enough to be my grandmother who, without a word, threw dust in my face. After that I knew nothing until my unfortunate decision to try to sit up while stuffed in the trunk of a car.

My heart clenched as I realized that the car had stopped. I needed to get out of here. My head hurt from where I had cracked it on the lid of the trunk, my limbs were cramping from being curled up for I didn't know how long, I needed to pee in the worst way, and there was a weird smell in this trunk that I did not want to think too closely about. As I scrubbed my hand over my face, I tried to pull my scattered thoughts together. There had to be a way out of here. I started feeling around to see if there was some kind of latch or lever I could use to open the trunk. I snatched my hand back suddenly when I felt something tear into my palm. Tears of pain and frustration sprang into my eyes. Why was this happening to me? As far as I knew I hadn't done anything wrong. I tried to live my life as quietly as possible. Things had been tough for me when my mother died, but I'd got through it. I was used to knowing I was all alone in the world, and I did the best I could. I blinked back the tears. I needed to get out of here. I started checking again, carefully using the one hand that wasn't injured. I stopped when I heard voices that seemed to be getting louder as people came closer to the car.

"Have you lost what is left of your mind? I am going to put you in a home, Grandma. That way at least the rest of the world can be protected from your particular brand of lunacy."

That didn't sound like something a kidnapper should be saying.

"You were supposed to be a moderating influence on Margot. This is one of the stupidest things you have ever done."

I heard a snort of laughter. "Sweetheart, you know that isn't even close to being true."

There was a pause in the conversation, and I tapped tentatively on the trunk lid.

"Uh, excuse me. I need some help. I think someone's made a mistake, but that's okay. I'm a very forgiving person." I thought hard for a second. "And forgetful. If you let me out, I'll forget this ever happened."

I heard a swift intake of breath. "She's awake. You kept her in the trunk and she's awake."

"Look, I really don't want to cause any trouble. I think you've made a big mistake, but if you can just let me out of here, I'm sure we can sort it out and nobody has to get in any trouble."

I heard the scraping of the key opening the trunk and slapped my uninjured hand over my eyes.

"Why do you have your hand over your face?"

"I don't know who you are. I can't identify you." I'd read enough crime thriller novels to know you never wanted to be a witness.

"You're being ridiculous. We're not going to hurt you."

I kept my hand exactly where it was. I wasn't sure if I believed the kidnapper with the friendly voice. I stiffened when I felt my hand being peeled away from my face, and I blinked as the light pierced my eyes.

"Hi."

The friendly voice belonged to a woman about my age whose defining feature seemed to be a tangled mane of red hair. If she wasn't one of my kidnappers, I would have said she had kind eyes and a sweet smile.

"I'm Tilda Atwill. Technically my name is Matilda, but everyone calls me Tilda. When I was eleven I tried to get people to call me Mattie, but it never caught on." She paused for a moment. "If you want to call me Mattie, that would be great."

I watched her, unsure what the correct response to this situation should be.

Tilda swallowed nervously and nodded her head in the direction of an older woman who was standing next to her. "And this is my grandmother, Maude. I'm really sorry about what she did but she's getting old and kind of losing it."

Maude pursed her lips. Even if I hadn't been told they were related I would have worked it out. They had the same round faces with out-of-control hair, although Maude's was gray rather than the fiery red. "I heard that."

"Oh, that you can hear, but when I told you we had to approach this situation with delicacy you obviously weren't paying attention."

Maude turned to Tilda and put her hands on her hips, her eyes firing sparks. "None of them were going to help us. We asked and they were ignoring us. What else did you expect me to do?"

"I expected you to be an adult and not come up with some insane idea that involved kidnapping an innocent woman."

Another voice piped up behind them and I could see a taller woman standing there, her gray hair clipped short in a pixie cut. "It was the only way for us to be sure she'd say yes."

"She didn't say yes," Tilda grated. "You just didn't give her the opportunity to say no." Tilda turned around and faced the older woman. "Let me guess. This was your idea, wasn't it, Margot?"

I closed my eyes in defeat. Great. Now I not only knew what all my kidnappers looked like, they had kindly provided their names. The very last thing that I wanted.

"Can I get out of here?"

Tilda looked flustered as she helped haul me out of the trunk. I stumbled against her as my legs hit the ground.

"You'll be okay," she murmured in my ear, still holding me against her as I got my bearings. "I promise."

I swallowed, unable to get the thick feeling out of my throat. "I live in Augusta. Can someone get me back there?"

Tilda looked at me sympathetically. "Augusta's only a couple of hours away. I'll drive you home as soon as I've dealt with this mess. I am so sorry."

For the first time since the trunk had been opened I saw a look of guilt on Maude's face. "She doesn't mean Augusta, Maine. She lives in Augusta, Georgia."

I started forward as Tilda's face grew red. I'm no doctor but I was pretty sure she looked like she was about to have a heart attack.

"Are you telling me that she has been locked in that trunk for a couple of days?"

"Closer to one day," Margot interjected. "We took turns driving and sleeping so we could get back here as quickly as possible. Also, we may not have stuck strictly to the speed limit. So, it was really a little less than one day."

"That does not make it better," Tilda hissed.

She let go of me and eyed me critically as I sagged back against the car, shocked at what I had just been told.

"You look like you're hungry. Maybe I should get you something to eat."

"You think getting me food is going to make me forget that your grandmother kidnapped me, threw me in a trunk and left me there for almost twenty-four hours while she drove me through at least half a dozen states…"

"It was closer to ten, we took a lot of back roads," Maude interrupted. "I thought you were a librarian. You should know that kind of information."

Tilda and I turned and glared at the woman who had managed to make both our lives that much more difficult.

"Sure, fine, get me some food."

2

_____

*W*ith help from Tilda, or Mattie, I still didn't understand half of the conversation we had just had, I stumbled up the stairs from the garage. As we made it to the top I remembered that I had a much more pressing need than food.

"I need to go to the bathroom," I mumbled.

"Of course, you do," Tilda said, her voice laced with sympathy.

She helped me to a small room at the back of the house and gently pushed me inside. After I'd finished, I studied the small window critically, wondering whether I'd be able to get through it.

A voice called out from beyond the door. "I would suggest you not try to get out through the window. It's a lot smaller than you think."

I opened the door. "How did you know?"

Tilda offered me an arm to lean on and I accepted it gratefully, still not entirely confident that my legs would continue supporting me. "When I was a teenager Grandma grounded me and I thought that I'd be able to get out through that window without her knowing. Having the fire department called to extract me was one of the humiliating lowlights of my life."

I tried hard to suppress the smile I could feel creeping across my face. If this wasn't a kidnapping, I could see how this woman and I could be friends. She helped me into the kitchen and sat me down at the table.

Tilda pushed her hair back from her face and gave me a gentle smile. She was definitely not acting like I would expect a kidnapper to act.

"What can I get you?" she asked.

"Some water would be good," I croaked.

"Of course," Tilda said before looking accusingly at the older women. "You've been stuffed in a trunk for twenty-four hours without any thought to your comfort."

Maude rolled her eyes. "Fine, I get it. We could have approached this situation more tactfully."

Tilda pointed a finger at her grandmother. "Not another word."

She handed over a glass of water and I drank it, the cold liquid soothing my throat. A tense silence descended on the room and I looked around cautiously, still unable to reconcile the fact that I had been kidnapped with the three women who looked like they couldn't harm a fly. Right up until Margot decided I was looking too comfortable.

"Did any of you see that documentary that screened last week?" She shook her head. "It was about a serial killer who owned a pig farm and was feeding the bodies to his pigs. Said it was the only way he was able to make a profit considering how much feed is costing these days."

"I'm guessing that wasn't the only reason that he was doing it." Maude looked as if she got those interesting nuggets of information every day.

Tilda was the only one registering the horrified look on

my face. "New rule, you two are not to say another word until we get…" she paused for a moment. "Wait a minute, who did you kidnap? She doesn't look like any of the photos of the people you were supposed to approach." Tilda flung a desperate glance at me. "And talk to. I swear, they were just supposed to talk to you."

"My name is Sadie Goodwin. I live in Augusta, Georgia and I work as a librarian."

"Nope. Not ringing a bell."

"It's complicated," Maude muttered.

We all looked at her expectantly.

"We're waiting," Tilda said, the warning obvious in her tone.

Maude hesitated. "She wasn't on the list."

Tilda's head dropped into her hands. "You kidnapped some random woman off the street. Why would you do that?"

Maude showed her first signs of nervousness. "I had a feeling that she was the one we needed."

"You had a feeling?"

I could do nothing but watch this discussion play out between the two women.

Tilda shook her head in confusion. There was a part of me that was glad I wasn't the only one.

I did latch on to one part of this conversation. I wasn't supposed to be taken. I stood up, filled with a new purpose. "It's obvious you made a mistake. If you could just point me towards the nearest door I will get out of your hair and you will never hear from me again." I was lying through my teeth. The second I got away from these people I was going to the police to suggest a psychiatric hold might be appropriate, if only to save the next innocent woman being randomly grabbed off the street.

Maude smiled sadly. "I'm afraid we can't do that. Even

though you weren't on the list, you are definitely supposed to be here. We really need your help."

"You kidnapped me because you need my help?" I sat back down heavily on the chair. "Aren't there better ways of asking for help that don't involve committing a felony?"

"You'd think so," Tilda sighed. "Look, a friend of ours is really sick." She paused as she swallowed and I could see a sheen of tears in her eyes. "To be honest, she's dying and we have a very short period of time to save her life."

"What do you mean, save her life? Isn't that what the doctors are supposed to do?"

"The doctors can't do anything for her. Her particular situation means that we need to find someone who is able to help her in a very specific way."

My mind started leaping forward from that statement, and I did not like where it was going. "You need me because you think I'm a match for this person."

Tilda nodded enthusiastically. "Exactly."

I got up and stood behind my chair, firmly gripping it. If this was going the way I thought it was going, I needed a weapon. "What exactly are you looking at me to donate?" In my mind I started calculating what parts of me could be valuable to someone who was dying. I was hoping it was blood or at worst bone marrow. Anything more than that and I was going to start swinging the chair around.

Tilda lifted her hands up in a placating gesture. "It's nothing like that." She stopped for a moment as her gaze narrowed at the point where my hands were gripping the chair.

"She's bleeding." Tilda turned to her grandmother. "Why is she bleeding?"

Maude shrugged. "Don't look at me. She was fine when we bundled her in the trunk."

Margot cleared her throat. "We did hit her head on the

door frame as we were carrying her out of the house." She glanced at me apologetically. "It took both of us to carry you. You're heavier than you look."

Great, just what I needed to hear to top off what was already a lousy day.

Tilda was keeping an eye on the bleeding. "I think we need to get a doctor to have a look at that. It looks deep."

I held up my hand to examine the gash that went across my palm. The blood was still flowing quite freely. It seemed, despite the fact that I had been kidnapped, I'd been the one to damage myself the most. "I cut it on something in the trunk, trying to find a way to get out."

Maude and Margot looked suitably chastened at my pathetic explanation.

"I'm going to get a doctor here to check it out," Tilda announced.

Maude cleared her throat. "We may have a problem with that."

Tilda paused as she went to grab her phone. "What else could possibly be going wrong now?"

"She doesn't exactly know what kind of town this is."

Tilda closed her eyes and I could see that she really wanted this day to end. "And by that you mean…?"

"She doesn't know who we are or what kind of people live here," Maude said firmly. "She can't see anyone until we explain that to her. If she reacts badly, we're all going to be in trouble."

I was fine with that. I could see that as far as kidnappings went, this had been a relatively easy one for me as the victim. I still didn't think they should get away with what they had done.

Tilda ran her hands through her hair and left the room. That wasn't good. I had been getting the feeling that she was the only sane one in the house. Before I had time to launch into a full-blown panic, she returned with a towel which she folded up and pressed down on the cut on my hand. She then led me back to my chair and sat me down. Keeping the pressure on my wound, she sat down next to me while Maude and Margot took seats on the opposite side of the table.

Tilda smiled at me in a way I knew was supposed to make me feel safe. It didn't.

"How open-minded are you?"

That did not sound good. "I guess I'm pretty open-minded," I said slowly. "But it depends what you're talking about."

"Do you believe in the possibility of UFOs?"

Okay, this had just taken a weird turn. "I guess they're possible. It isn't something I've spent a great deal of time thinking about."

"How about psychics?"

"Yet again, not something I spend a lot of time contemplating. Why are you asking me these things?"

Tilda ran her hands through her hair. "I'm just trying to work out how you're going to react to something that might be a little surprising at first."

I was getting ready to snap. "The longer you dance around the topic, the less open-minded I become."

Tilda swallowed nervously and the grip on my hand tightened. "We're witches. We live in a town which has other paranormal beings, and we need to know that if you walk out that door that you are not going to freak out if the first person you come across is a troll."

"And that's the point," I said as I pulled my hand out of Tilda's solicitous grip and stood up.

"What point?" asked Maude.

"The point where it finally gets through my thick head that you people are insane." I took in a shaky breath. "You would have thought that just being kidnapped by you was enough for me to reach that conclusion. Or the fact that I still have a sneaking suspicion that you're going to try to force me to donate a kidney to your sick friend."

"Stealing human organs is more common than you think," Margot said, pulling all the attention to herself. "I watched a documentary about it last month."

I sucked in a breath. "Or that one of my kidnappers keeps talking about things like serial killers and organ harvesters."

"I was just trying to lighten the mood," pouted Margot.

"Seriously not helping," murmured Tilda.

"Fine." I slammed my good hand down on the table. "You want me to believe you're a witch? Prove it. Conjure up something. In fact, you still haven't fed me. I wouldn't mind a chicken salad sandwich."

Tilda sighed. "That isn't the way magic works."

I rolled my eyes. "Of course, it isn't."

"You think magic is easy? The effort and energy that goes into creating a spell is draining. You don't just wiggle your nose or click your fingers and something appears. We're not genies, you know." She paused for a moment. "Not that there's anything wrong with genies. They are valuable members of the community."

Margot snorted. "You can't say a bad thing about anyone, can you? Everyone knows that genies are malevolent beings, but you just can't bring yourself to admit it." She looked over at me. "A genie will never grant you a wish that will come out like you wanted. There's always some sting in the tail to punish you for even contemplating asking them to use their magic." She leaned forward and narrowed her eyes as if she was imparting the secrets of the universe to me. "Never trust a genie's wish."

Sure. That was the important lesson I was going to take away from today.

hy was I not running through the door and screaming for the closest police officer? Any sane person would be trying to get away from these people as soon as they could, but for some unknown reason I was rooted to the spot waiting for proof of the impossible. As I watched Tilda and Margot arguing over the best way to prove to me that magic existed in the world, and whether genies were truly evil, that became my biggest question. I was pretty sure that most other kidnap victims wouldn't have a problem bringing the full force of the law down on what had become a truly absurd situation. I glanced over at Maude and found her watching me carefully. While Tilda and Margot were doing the worst job in the world of trying to convince me that the paranormal community did exist and that I had just landed waist deep in the middle of it, Maude was studying my every move. As I was contemplating the ludicrousness of my situation, she started to stare at her own hand. A small light sphere started to form in her palm. From where I was sitting it looked like a dark blue ball with flashes of lightning spinning at a fast rate, like a miniature electrical storm.

"How are you doing that?" I asked hoarsely.

Tilda and Margot stopped their discussion on the benefits and faults of genies.

Tilda rolled her eyes. "Well sure, that's one way of showing her, but she wanted a chicken salad sandwich."

"How is she doing that?" I repeated. The mind splintering terror that I had left behind in the trunk, when I first started to realize that my kidnappers may not be the vicious thugs I had originally feared, came rushing back.

"Grandma is an elemental witch," Tilda said in a matter-of-fact manner. "Elemental witches are able to affect things like weather and, at a much smaller level, are able to create balls of lightning.

"Of course they can," I muttered as I stared at the spinning sphere that all reason told me shouldn't exist.

Maude closed her hand with a snap and the ball winked out of existence. "I think you should call the doctor now."

"Sure, I'll get right on that," Tilda said as she watched me warily. She pushed Margot towards me. "Catch her if she starts to faint."

"I try that and she's liable to squash me," Margot muttered. "She's not exactly the delicate type."

I stayed standing with my back against the wall, still trying to make sense of what was happening. As far as I could tell I wasn't in any immediate danger. I just needed to start getting control of my situation and finding the fastest and safest way out of it.

"Where am I?" I blurted out.

Maude smiled as if she knew what I was trying to accomplish. Considering what I had already seen her do I wasn't far off believing that she could read my mind. Of course, they could have drugged me and that was why I was seeing things.

"You're in Walker Bay. We're a smallish town on the coast of Maine. Like Tilda said, just a couple of hours from Augusta."

"Are you going to hurt me?"

The look in Maude's eyes softened. "We would never hurt you. All we're asking is for you to listen to what we have to say with an open mind. I know this has to be terrifying for you, and I understand that we probably went about this in the worst way possible. Once the doctor has fixed up your hand we will sit down with you and explain everything."

"What will happen to me after that?"

Maude heaved a sigh and for the first time she looked like an elderly woman who was carrying a burden that was becoming too much for her to bear. "After that you are free to do what you want. If you want to walk away, you can."

"But you're hoping I'll stay," I said softly.

Maude looked me in the eyes. "I am hoping, praying, and wishing that you will stay and help us, because if you don't, I may lose my best friend, and I have no idea how I am going to face that."

Great. As long as there was no pressure.

I jumped at the sound of knocking at the front door.

Tilda had re-entered the kitchen and she was wringing her hands. "The doctor's here," she announced.

"Are you planning on letting him in?" asked Margot.

"I don't know whether we should." The plaintive expression on Tilda's face showed how uncertain she was about the situation.

"What's the problem?" I asked.

"I don't know if we've managed to convince you about us being witches, and there being other beings that don't conform to your view of what constitutes normal in the world," Maude said. "We don't really have time for you to catch up and be comfortable with what we're telling you.

When we open that door, you're going to get more proof than you know what to do with. We need you to not react to what you see. No matter how fantastical the next half hour is to you, we need you to keep calm and not question anything. If you show in any way that you are in a paranormal town and you don't know the first thing about this world, there will be consequences." She paused for a second. "For all of us. We made a choice because we were desperate, and I understand fully if you want us punished for what we did, but just know that there will be consequences for you as well."

The three women watched me keenly as if each of them was trying to see how I would react.

"Can you do this?" Tilda asked earnestly. "We need to know now, before this goes any further."

I nodded my head, unwilling to speak. I could do this. If it got me closer to finding out what these people wanted from me, and possibly getting out of here safely, I could do anything.

"Okay," Tilda mumbled to herself. "Let's get this over and done with."

I waited as she went to the front door. I heard murmuring as she greeted the visitors and then I heard clattering on the wooden floors. I chewed on my lower lip, playing in my mind everything that I had been told so far. There was still a part of me that was having some issues believing what I had already seen and been told. I was having trouble understanding why a part of me wanted to trust these women. Maybe I'd hit my head a little harder than I thought.

Margot and Maude kept throwing worried looks in my direction, so I knew that whoever was coming through that door was going to test everything I believed. I just had to be calm and deal with it. I could do this.

Despite mentally trying to prepare myself, I almost

passed out when I saw who had followed Tilda into the kitchen. I felt the blood drain from my face, and I could tell by the way that Margot moved closer to me that she had resigned herself to getting squashed as she tried to soften my descent into oblivion. The doctor towered over Tilda. It was fortunate the house had high ceilings or he would have been uncomfortably close to hitting his head. He had dark hair that was shot through with silver, gentle eyes, wore a white lab coat and carried a battered leather doctor's bag. All of this was something that I would normally expect, although the fact this town had a doctor that still did house calls would usually strike me as odd. Today it didn't because I was a little overwhelmed by the fact that the doctor had the body of a horse. My mind started casting around, trying to remember the name for the half human, half horse creature that I remembered from the book of myths my mother had read to me as a child. Centaur. That was it. I'd always wondered how they would go about their lives split between the human world and the animal world. Apparently, they became doctors. I bit harder on my lip, suppressing an over-whelming urge to giggle.

"This is our friend, Sadie," Tilda said, as she did a terrible job of hiding her nervousness. "She came to visit and she's managed to cut herself."

"And hit her head," Margot added.

"Twice," I murmured, impressed that I had regained control of my voice.

The centaur smiled, his white teeth gleaming like a dentist's commercial. I wondered if he ate human food or grass. I bit my lip again to prevent me from asking stupid questions. I was going to need an icepack after the doctor left. He stood in front of me and leaned down as I tried to regulate my breathing and not hyperventilate.

"My name is Dr Collias, and this is my assistant

Marigold." He gestured towards the young woman who had followed him into the house. With the shock of seeing a centaur, I hadn't noticed her entrance. She smiled in a way that was gentle and calming. I smiled back at her, grateful for a moment of normal. Dr Collias put his bag on the table, reached in and pulled out a pair of glasses. "Now let's have a look at that cut."

I tentatively held my hand out as he perched the glasses on the end of his nose. The moment was so surreal I had to stifle the hysteria that was bubbling inside me. His hands were surprisingly soft as he examined my wound.

"That looks like you've cut it deep. How did you do it?"

"A piece of metal," I said vaguely.

"You're going to need stitches for this one." He turned around and started pulling things out of his bag.

I noticed Marigold also had a doctor's bag, although it looked much newer. She had placed it on the table and was pulling out small glass jars with various powders in them that I'd never seen before. She pulled out a clay bowl which had markings on the outside that I couldn't interpret. What she didn't pull out of her bag was anything that resembled a medical instrument. I glanced at Tilda with what I was sure was a panicked look on my face. She stepped towards me, grabbed my other hand and squeezed. Dr Collias glanced at us with a quizzical expression on his face.

"Sadie hates needles," Tilda explained.

I had no problem with needles. I never did. My problem was with the mythical creature that was wielding the needle. I winced slightly as the first needle with the local anesthetic entered my hand and watched as the doctor deftly stitched up the jagged cut. When he lifted up his head I marveled at the small neat stitches.

"The stitches will need to come out in a week. When was your last tetanus shot?"

I stopped and tried to remember. I was the kind of kid who spent her childhood with her nose in a book. I didn't do anything adventurous enough to warrant a tetanus shot, and I hadn't changed as I grew older. "I don't remember."

"Better have one, just in case there was something nasty on that piece of metal. Can you roll up your sleeve, please?"

I let go of Tilda's hand and rolled up my sleeve. This time I didn't wince when the needle went in. Hopefully that meant I was dealing better with this whole situation.

"Now Marigold is going to bandage your hand with a poultice. That will help with the healing process. Treat it as you would any other poultice and we'll leave extra salve so you can reapply and bandage again later tonight."

I had no idea what that meant, or what I had to do, but I'd keep my mouth shut and let Tilda translate when the doctor and his assistant left.

As the doctor moved away, his assistant stepped forward to take his place. I had to stop myself from snatching away my hand as she slathered the strange smelling concoction that she had prepared in the clay bowl onto the stitched-up wound. This did not seem like a normal thing to do.

"So where are these bumps on your head?" the doctor asked.

I pointed to the top of my forehead where I had hit the lid of the trunk.

He felt the top of my head. "Bit of a bump there but it doesn't seem too bad. How about the other one?"

That stumped me. My other head injury had happened while I was unconscious during my kidnapping.

"That was more to the back of her skull," Margot added helpfully while pointing to her own head.

"Thank you," Dr Collias said with a quizzical smile on his face. "How exactly did you do this?"

"I'm a bit clumsy," I mumbled, perfectly aware that I had

stepped over into Stockholm Syndrome territory. There was no other reason for me to be protecting my kidnappers, but the appearance of the centaur had turned my world view upside down. I was going to cling to the slightly familiar, even if they appeared to be insane.

"Really?" Dr Collias asked.

Even I could hear the skepticism in his voice.

"She's had a rough day," Tilda said quietly, with what I considered was the understatement of the year.

"All done," announced Marigold as she finished wrapping my hand. Despite my concerns about the poultice I had to admit that it felt soothing against my skin.

I could feel Dr Collias watching me intently and I looked up at him. "Is there anything else that I should be aware of?"

His deep brown eyes were hypnotic and, for a moment, I badly wanted to tell him everything, but I remembered Maude's warning about consequences. Somehow, I didn't think those consequences would be something I was comfortable with. I shook my head. It looked like I was going with the devil I knew.

"Very well then. If you have any issues, please feel free to call me."

As Tilda walked the medical professionals out, I sat still in the chair.

"You can start breathing now," Maude said as we heard the front door close.

"What the hell have you done to me?" I sniffed the gooey mess on my hand. "What is this?"

"That is a healing poultice," Margot said haughtily. "Marigold is the most talented healing witch in the coven. The salve she makes will take days off the healing time for that cut."

I needed to get this straight. "So, the centaur is a proper doctor and the woman assisting him is a witch."

"Yes."

Such a simple answer for a really complicated situation. "I have a head injury, don't I?"

"Why do you say that?" asked Tilda as she returned to the room. "The doctor said your head looked okay."

"Because that is the only explanation for the fact that I think my doctor has the body of a horse."

"Dr Collias is a centaur and a highly respected member of this community," Tilda said primly. "Just because you are not used to seeing his species does not mean that he doesn't exist."

I looked up at the ceiling. "I can't believe how weird this day has been."

Maude cleared her throat. "Unfortunately, it isn't going to get any better."

"Why?" I asked suspiciously. I was pretty sure that if I was hallucinating from a head injury enough that I believed my doctor was a centaur, things couldn't get much worse."

The three women looked at each other, as if worried about my reaction. That was unfair. I was pretty sure that I'd been the most cooperative kidnapping victim they were likely to come across.

Maude put on a smile that I knew was supposed to put me at ease. It didn't. "The reason we kidnapped you, in fact the reason we found you at all is because you're probably a witch too."

Of course, I was.

4

"*N*ow, why on Earth would you think I'm a witch?"

Tilda decided to take on the role of calming the panicked kidnapped victim. "The most obvious reason is that if you weren't a witch you would be curled up in a ball on the ground, paralyzed with fear."

"What are you talking about?"

"Walker Bay is protected by wards that have been reinforced through the years. If a non-paranormal tries to get through the borders they are struck with a feeling of dread and they can't help but turn away. You don't seem to be paralyzed by dread or fear."

"I think you're underestimating your grandmother's effect on me. And anyway, what kind of a name is Walker Bay for a magic town? Shouldn't it be something like Bewitched Cove or Cauldron Falls?"

Tilda smiled tightly. I could tell she was having a bad day, but at this stage I wasn't inclined to go out of my way to make it easier. "It's called Walker Bay because the first paranormal who settled here was Marion Walker."

"That seems to be a bit of an underwhelming story."

"Just because we're magical doesn't make us that different from everybody else. We're just trying to live our lives the best way we can."

"And that includes dragging me here against my will."

"You're right," Maude said unexpectedly.

"I am?" That surprised me.

"We shouldn't have taken you the way we did. We should have asked you for help."

"What is it you want from me?" All of a sudden, I knew that I didn't care about the rest. I was going to put the whole paranormal situation into a box and revisit it later. Much later. What I really needed to know was why I had been taken from my quiet, peaceful life and dropped into the middle of a freak show.

Maude clasped her hands together. "As we've told you, we are all witches."

That was the part I wanted to ignore for now, so I nodded, as if in agreement.

"We belong to a coven that's based here in Walker Bay. There are two covens in this town, but we are considered the strongest and our leader sits on the Council."

"What's the Council?" I asked.

"Kind of like our governing body," Tilda said. "The Council is made up of paranormals who are considered leaders of the various races. They run this town. It is considered the ultimate honor to be on the Council. Flora Harstone is our coven leader and she has a strong voice on the Council. It gives our coven a position of authority, not just here in Walker Bay, but in all the paranormal communities in the country."

The fact that there were more of these towns out there and this wasn't an anomaly, was another thing I was going to put in that box. "That still doesn't explain why I'm here."

Maude took in a breath and I was surprised to see a sheen

of tears in her eyes. "Over the last couple of months Flora has been deteriorating both mentally and physically."

"Okay, I'm still not seeing how that is my problem."

"Two weeks ago, we believe she overdosed on a sleeping potion."

"Accidentally or on purpose?" I asked.

"Accidentally, of course," Maude replied, her lips quivering.

"You're not sure, are you?"

Tilda put a comforting hand on her grandmother's arm. "No, we're not sure. Sometimes powerful witches are prone to mental issues. We had some concerns that might have happened to Flora."

"What does that have to do with me?"

"She's still unconscious." Tilda's eyes were bright with unshed tears. "In these situations, where there's a possibility of a deliberate overdose, we need to find somebody with a link to her to take part in a healing ceremony."

"What kind of link?" I couldn't help the suspicion coloring my voice.

"A magical link. Usually it's a close friend or a family member. Sometimes it's just someone with a certain kind of magical power."

Okay, this had gone on far enough. "I'm really sorry about your friend, and I wish I could help, but I have never shown any kind of magical ability in my life. What made you think that I was the person you were looking for?"

"You can help us," insisted Maude. "I'm sure of it." She paused for a moment. "Does anyone in your family have magical ability? It's usually strongest through the female line."

I shook my head. "I've never suspected that witches that could do magic actually existed. I thought people who called themselves witches were all nature-loving hippie chicks who needed an excuse to dance around naked under the full moon."

"Oh, we do that," Margot interrupted.

I looked over at Tilda who was grimacing. "It's a choice. Not all of us do it."

"Until today I had never seen anything that made me believe that the paranormal could possibly exist. To be honest, I'm still not sure this isn't some hallucination caused by hitting my head."

"Let's go with the theory you're not hallucinating." I could tell Maude was trying to be patient with me. "Even though performing most magic is a learned process, witches need to have some innate ability that they are born with. Usually this ability manifests itself during your teenage years, but in rare cases it can happen later with a bit of help. Have you ever realized you knew something that you couldn't possibly know? Did you get minor injuries which seemed to heal quicker than they should have? Were there slight weather fluctuations based on your mood?"

"I have had nothing like that. Right up until you kidnapped me, my life was perfectly normal."

"Did you ever see your mother do anything that you couldn't really explain? Just think carefully. It could have been something small."

I shook my head. "There was nothing." I could see Maude was getting frustrated, but I just couldn't give her the answer she so desperately wanted.

"It could be your father," mused Tilda. "Although magic usually runs through the female line, sometimes it can come through the male line, just not as strongly."

I grimaced. "My father was one of that special breed of men who would sneak out on a one-night stand before the sun had come up."

"Oh," Tilda said quietly. I could see she was trying to come up with an appropriate response. "Those guys suck."

"That they do," I replied, remembering the incredibly awkward conversation I'd had with my mother about how I came to bless her life. Her words, not mine.

"Did your mom know anything about him?"

"He told her that his name was Jasper, but I'm not putting a great deal of faith in his ability to be honest about even the most basic of details."

"He could have been telling the truth about that," Maude interjected.

I noticed the sudden gleam in her eye. "You know who he is." I tried really hard to keep the interested tone out of my voice. I had long ago given up on ever finding out who my father was. Mostly, I didn't care to know. Hard to see the good side of a man who didn't even have the guts to stick around for his sexual partner to wake up. Despite that, there was still a small part of me that was curious.

Maude settled into her seat. "Flora was the youngest of three sisters. She was a surprise for the family, and for witches surprises are pretty damn rare. Collette was seventeen when Flora was born, and Dinah was sixteen, so they didn't really have much interest in the new baby in the family. Flora's mother Bessie was leading the coven at that stage, so she didn't have a lot of time for a newborn. Collette and Dinah were starting their own lives. As a result, Flora pretty much raised herself with a bit of help from my mother."

"Where was their father?" I asked, curious at the way the men seemed to be ignored in this story.

"Bessie's husband died when Collette and Dinah were young. Nobody has much of an idea who Flora's father was." Maude took a breath. "Collette was always expected to lead the coven after their mother stepped down. She was trained

27

for it from the first day she could utter an incantation. Succession in a coven is always planned out meticulously. A coven without strong leadership is at best, ineffectual. At worst it is dangerous. On the night Bessie Harstone was to turn over leadership of the coven to Collette, the Seer stepped in and named thirteen-year-old Flora as the leader."

"What's a Seer?" I interrupted.

"A Seer is a witch who has the gift of prophecy," Tilda took over the story. "Fortune telling is a pretty standard skill for witches. You want to know if you'll get that promotion or land the hot guy in class, any witch with basic skills can tell you that. The thing is that fortune telling is personal and fluid. It is your future if you continue on a set path, but it can be affected by little things. Your fortune tells you you're going to land that promotion, so you feel confident enough to be a little less circumspect about your behavior at work. HR gets involved. Next thing you know, promotion's gone. Seer's are rare and very different. They see the big picture and when they have a prophecy it stands as a kind of landmark that the rest of the world rotates around. When a Seer proclaims a prophecy, witches follow it to the letter."

"Are you telling me that despite Collette having trained her whole life for the position, she was passed over for a teenager? And the coven just went for it?" I was having a little trouble understanding witch politics.

Maude took up the story again. "Nobody expected it, least of all Collette and Flora. I was there that night. Collette kept saying that it had to be a mistake. She was livid. Imagine spending your whole life training for your destiny only to have it ripped away at the last moment and given to a child."

"How did Flora react to it?"

Maude smiled as she remembered. "She was serene, the way Flora always is. She wasn't grasping for it, she simply accepted it. The rest of the coven descended into chaos. It fractured that day. Some stayed and others left, afraid that the coven would be compromised by being led by a child. Collette and Dinah were the first to leave." Maude blinked back a couple of tears. "The way everything disintegrated broke Bessie's heart. She died soon after and Collette and Dinah left town straight after the funeral."

"How does this relate to my father?" I asked.

"Collette took her family with her, including her nine-year-old son, Jasper. That was forty years ago which would fit in with the timeline we're looking at."

"You think this Jasper could be my father, and that would mean Collette would be my grandmother."

"And that would make Flora your great-aunt. It explains why I felt your magic would match Flora's."

I scrubbed my hands over my face. "So, let's get this straight. My mother is human…"

"As far as we know," said Tilda.

"That woman worked two back-breaking jobs to keep me fed and clothed. Trust me when I say there was no hint of magic in our lives."

"Okay,"

"If I have any magic in me at all, it must come from my father, and you've already told me that males are not as powerful as the female line."

"True," murmured Maude.

"If that's the case, my magic, if we can even trigger it to manifest in me, will most likely be so diluted to be almost useless." I put up my hand as Tilda tried to interrupt. "I'm being realistic. You're scraping the bottom of the barrel here."

"I think you're wrong," Maude said quietly. "Margot and I had no reason to go to Georgia. There were no other people on the list anywhere near you, but we were drawn there." She grasped my hand in hers. "As soon as I saw you coming out of the library, I knew you were the one that we needed. I felt it, deep inside. It's one of the reasons I was able to talk Margot into just grabbing you, rather than talking to you like we tried with the rest of the candidates."

"Like it would have taken much to talk Margot into participating in a kidnapping." The exasperation in Tilda's voice indicated that despite her annoyance, she was not entirely surprised at the events that led to my current situation.

"What's this list you keep talking about?" I asked.

"When Flora first got sick, we came up with a list of family members who might be able to help. We've been visiting those that are close by asking for assistance." Maude had a distasteful look on her face.

"I'm guessing none of them were willing to step up to the plate."

"You could say that," Maude spat out.

"Collette threatened to call the police on us," Margot added.

"Great," said Tilda. "The woman who's likely to be her grandmother threatened to call the police when you knocked on her door and asked for help. If Collette finds out you kidnapped her granddaughter and brought her from Georgia to Maine in the trunk of a car, she'll call in the National Guard."

"I think you mean FBI," I interrupted. "The FBI works on kidnapping cases across state lines."

Maude rolled her eyes. "Didn't know how many states we passed through, but you can tell me about federal law enforcement jurisdiction."

"Are you going to help us?" asked Tilda.

"I don't know if I can. What you're expecting of me seems so much bigger than what I am capable of doing."

Maude smiled gently. "You need to have faith. We were drawn to you for a reason."

They kept saying that, but I still had my doubts. I took a deep breath and looked around the room at the three women who seemed to believe that I could achieve the impossible. There was fear in their eyes, and I could see they were terrified that I would say no. To be honest, a part of me was tempted to do just that. I had no business being anywhere near a magical community. This was so far outside my sense of normal as to be ridiculous. But what if it wasn't? What if this woman really was my aunt? The part of me that had watched as my mother, my only family member, was lowered into the ground, ached to know the truth. It was possible I needed these people as much as they needed me.

"Maybe you're right, but before I decide, I think I should meet Flora Harstone."

5

*A*s we traveled to Flora's house, I was grateful that I had already been introduced to Dr Collias. Shocking as it had been to meet a centaur, it had at least lessened the impact of what I saw when we left Maude's home. Being in the front seat of Maude's car, rather than the trunk, meant that this time I had an unimpeded view of Walker Bay, and I had to admit that nothing could have prepared me for what I saw.

Although I had been kidnapped from Georgia, it was not my home state. My upbringing could be best described as nomadic. My childhood had seen my mom moving us from one small town to another all over the country. As an adult I had continued this behavior, unable to feel at home in any one place, so I had seen a lot of towns in my life. Architecturally, this town looked no different from those that I'd seen. There was a collection of old and new buildings to show how the town had grown over the years. The people, on the other hand, looked very different. Centaurs weren't quite as rare as I thought they would be. The coloring on people included a variety of grays and greens. Heights varied widely. There was no way that I would be able to name what the majority of the creatures walking down the street even were. I could understand why the town had put up wards to prevent non-magical people from entering the township. There would have been no other way that this community would have been protected.

"You need to stop gawking," Tilda mentioned from the back seat.

"I'm not gawking," I muttered. I was totally gawking.

"You cannot let anyone know that you aren't a part of the paranormal community," Tilda insisted. "Just act like you know exactly what's going on. Never ask anyone what they are or how much magic they have."

That was going to be hard. "What if one of them decides to kill me, or eat me, or something."

If she hadn't been driving, I was sure that Maude would have dropped her head in frustration. "Walker Bay has all the same laws as the rest of the country. We also have a sheriff's department that is staffed by competent law enforcement officials."

Tilda snorted. "That wasn't what you said when Deputy Iversen pulled you over for speeding."

"Deputy Iversen has let his position go to his head. I was barely going over the limit."

"Course you were," snickered Tilda.

"So, all the laws are the same?" I asked.

Maude nodded. "We have a few extra laws that are tailored to the county and the kind of people we have here. Various items used for spells are restricted, and some cultural sensitivities are catered for, but all the main laws are based on the law of the land. If there wasn't, there would be anarchy. Murder is still murder, regardless of whether a gun is used or witchcraft."

That made sense. It also made this whole situation slightly less terrifying.

When we pulled up to the house, I was surprised. When you get told that you are visiting the house of a coven leader, there are some expectations. This house did not meet those expectations. It was a simple cottage that looked to be over seventy years old, set back from the road and surrounded by forest. I squinted my eyes and looked more carefully at the forest. The trees that surrounded the cottage seemed to be leaning towards it, as if in a protective stance. I looked over in confusion at Tilda and she nodded. I guess I was going to need to be a lot more open in my view of the world, because up until this moment I would have said that what I was seeing was absolutely impossible.

The front door opened and an almost exact replica of Margot walked out on to the porch.

I looked over at Margot with a raised eyebrow.

"My twin sister, Isobel."

"Yep, there's two of them," murmured Tilda.

This day was just getting better with every step.

"Who the hell is she?" barked Isobel.

"She's here to help," Maude replied with a soothing tone to her voice that concerned me. If Isobel was more volatile than the woman who easily discussed serial killings and organ harvesting, then I'd rather keep my distance from her.

"That still doesn't tell me who she is."

"This is Sadie Goodwin. We have reason to believe that she may be related to Flora."

"Sadie Goodwin." Isobel screwed her face up as if concentrating hard. "I don't remember that name being on the list."

"She wasn't on the list," Maude said through gritted teeth.

"Whose bright idea was it to deviate from the list? We had the list for a reason. Did you just snatch some random woman off the street?"

"That's exactly what they did." I would say that I was starting to get annoyed, but I had flown past annoyed hours ago. "Now, I've been having a really bad day. The only reason I am not screaming for the police is because I've been told there is some woman who may be related to me who needs my help."

Isobel's mouth dropped open. "You have got to be kidding me." She glared at Margot. "Have you lost your mind?"

Finally, someone who seemed to understand the gravity of the situation. "Lady, I am with you one hundred percent. Now could we please do this. I'm hurt, I'm tired and I haven't had anything to eat for I don't know how long. I just want to see this woman and hopefully we can work out the next step after that."

Isobel paused for a moment and her eyes seemed to be appraising me. I wasn't sure what she saw, but she turned around and walked back in the house.

Tilda came up behind me. "We can go in now."

"What's her deal?" I muttered as we stepped up to the porch.

"Isobel has the job of protecting Flora until she can be cured. She and Flora have always been close." Tilda sighed. "We had a plan."

"The list." Everything came back to that damn list. At some point I was hoping to get my hands on it. If I really was part of this family, I wanted to find out who else there was. After spending my entire life with my mother being my only relation, the idea that I had an entire extended family was enough to blow my mind. Not quite as much as the paranormal bloodline in the family, but close.

As we went to enter the house, Tilda put her hand on my arm. "Don't make any sudden moves towards Flora."

"Why?"

"Remember what I said about Isobel and Flora being close."

I nodded wordlessly.

"If you make a move that looks threatening to Flora, Isobel will slit your throat. Margot may sound like the scary twin but she's all talk. Isobel is the one you need to be careful around."

Okay, I was going to remember that. Although I was still a little reluctant to see Margot as being the safe twin.

We followed Isobel into a bedroom at the back of the house. There were candles flickering around the room, their glow bouncing off the walls in an otherworldly light. In the middle of the room was Flora Harstone lying on the bed. If I didn't know any better, I would have thought she was sleeping. She was bathed in a blue light that encapsulated her like a second skin. I looked down at the woman who was possibly my aunt. After years of believing my mother and I were alone in this world, it was a bit of a shock to discover I might have family. As I reached to touch her arm, a ribbon of blue light seemed to emanate from her body and wrapped itself around my hand.

"What is that?" I asked, unwilling to move.

Maude gave the first real smile I had seen. "That's proof that we were right. You are her family and you can help her."

"The blue light says that?"

Maude nodded. "The blue light means her aura recognizes you and is reaching out to you. If I had any doubts at all that you were the one we needed, that just blew them all away."

I stayed still as the ribbon of light danced up and down my arm. The sensation felt warm and I felt safe. I didn't understand why, but I felt like I had come home.

I glanced over at Maude. "I know you said she took a

sleeping potion, but what did the doctor say was wrong with her exactly?"

Maude shifted uncomfortably and glanced at Margot. "We didn't call in the doctor."

"Why ever not? I had a lousy cut on the hand, and you insisted on getting a doctor for me."

"We know it was the sleeping potion," Isobel interrupted, her voice gruff and defensive. "We don't need a doctor to tell us that."

"Are you one hundred percent sure of that?" I asked. "Maybe what is wrong with her is medical and you have left her like this for the last couple of weeks. She could die and it would have absolutely nothing to do with taking an overdose. Ever thought that it could be a stroke or something like that."

For the first time the women looked uncertain. I tried another tack. "Are you one hundred percent sure that this was caused by the sleeping potion and not by some illness?"

All four women shook their heads.

"So, you're not one hundred percent sure what magic was used, but you're confident enough to assume that it isn't something medical." I paused for a moment. "Are any of you a doctor or a nurse? How about an EMT? At this stage I'd even be accepting of basic first aid."

"We'd know," insisted Isobel. "There would have been some sign if it was medical, but we found her in the morning with an empty bottle of the sleeping potion and I know it was full the night before. And then her aura snapped out and enveloped her body. That's always a sign that magic is involved."

I tried a different tack. "Okay, I concede that you would know about potions and spells better than me, but couldn't the doctor tell you what kind of physical effects whatever this is could be having on her body? For all we know, the potion could have caused brain damage." I wondered when I had become so pessimistic. I'd always thought of myself as a glass half full person. Amazing how being kidnapped could change your outlook on life.

The women paused as if considering what I was saying, so I decided to play the next of kin card. "I want the doctor called in."

Maude shook her head. "I don't know whether that is a good idea. We need to keep this as quiet as possible. Flora has kept her position on the Council because she has not shown a moment of weakness since she was thirteen years old. It's why we didn't tell anyone she was having episodes before she took the sleeping potion. If the other coven discovers what has happened to her, they'll make a move against her. We've kept this information strictly between the four of us. We can't trust anyone else."

"You don't trust the doctor you just had sewing up my hand?" I queried.

"Of course, we do, but this is different."

"How? This seems to be a medical emergency. If, as you say, the doctor is bound by the same rules as the rest of the country, he can't say anything."

"I don't like it," stated Isobel.

Of course, she didn't.

Isobel narrowed her eyes. "How do we even know that you're her family? You've never tried to contact her. And then you just turn up when she's at her weakest."

After everything I'd been through today, getting attacked for not contacting Flora was not the way to go. Even Margot winced at Isobel's comment.

"Until about an hour ago, I didn't even know that you people existed. Now I have blue lights running up and down my arm. You either accept that I'm her family or you don't.

Just please make a decision because you still haven't fed me, and I just want this done so I can find something to eat."

"I'm calling Dr Collias," announced Tilda as she pulled out her phone. "If we were less worried about protecting the coven and thinking a bit more clearly, we would have done this earlier. I'll make sure he comes alone."

I looked down at Flora's face as Tilda made the call. Maybe this woman was my aunt. If she was, it was my job to keep her safe. Starting now.

This time when a centaur came through the door, I am pleased to say I handled it much better. I even managed to give Dr Collias a small smile and received one in return.

"I didn't expect to see you so soon. Are you experiencing any more symptoms?"

I must have given him a confused look.

"With your head. Any nausea, or is the headache worsening?"

You'd better believe the headache was worsening. Unfortunately, it was for a completely different reason than what the doctor was expecting.

Maude stepped forward. "You're not here to check on Sadie, Ambrose."

The centaur was called Ambrose. Not what I would have guessed.

"On the last full moon, Flora drank a large bottle of sleeping potion and we haven't been able to wake her up. We believe her issue is magical, but it has been brought to our attention that we should have a medical opinion before tackling the magical side of the problem."

Dr Collias opened his mouth, closed it and swallowed, before trying again. "Who suggested getting me to check her out?"

Maude gestured in my direction. "As part of the healing spell we require a magical match, preferably a family member to take part in the spell. As you are aware, Flora is estranged from her family and none of them were willing to help. We grabbed Sadie because we think she may be Flora's niece. She has agreed to help us."

"Grabbed?" queried Dr Collias.

"Fine, if you want to be pedantic, we kidnapped her. I threw a spell ball in her face to knock her out and we loaded her in the trunk. That's how she got hurt."

The horrified look on Dr Collias's face was something to behold. "So, let me get this straight. Not only did you not come to me the second you discovered that one of my oldest and dearest friends is in a coma, you went out and abducted one of her family members, and then made me an unwitting accomplice to a federal crime."

Yes, what they'd done was as bad as I thought.

"She's fine with it now," Tilda said, hurriedly.

"I don't know if fine is the term I'd use," I muttered. "More like, I can see the bigger picture."

Dr Collias rubbed a hand over his face and glanced at me. "Do you want me to report this to law enforcement?"

A part of me really wanted to do that. I kept thinking that this was not the way that a kidnapping victim should be acting. I should be doing everything I could to get away from these people and, despite my surprise when introduced to Dr Collias, my instincts told me that he was a good man... centaur...whatever. I could tell that if I said the word he would get me out of here and somewhere safe. But, like I said before, I was beginning to see the bigger picture in all this.

"No, I want you to examine Flora and let us know what is happening with her. My situation is not going to change in the near future. I'm concerned that hers might."

"Very well, but we are going to have a serious talk about this when I am finished."

I was pretty sure that was aimed more at my kidnappers than me. From the way Tilda paled, I could see they weren't looking forward to that talk.

"I need some privacy while I do the examination."

"I'm staying." Isobel stepped forward and there was no way I was going to argue with her.

"No, if anyone stays, it is going to be Sadie." Collias glared at Isobel. He was obviously used to the way the coven worked, although from the way he was looking at them, his world view of these women had taken a serious battering in the past few minutes. "If she is the next of kin, as you say, she has the most right to be here."

Isobel opened her mouth to argue, but Maude stepped forward and placed a hand on her arm. "That's acceptable. We trust you to take care of Flora, regardless of your feelings regarding our actions."

The women moved out of the house with Isobel muttering. "I didn't kidnap anyone. Why am I being punished?"

"You okay?" Collias asked as I followed him into Flora's bedroom.

"I'm fine. A little out of my depth, but fine."

He proceeded to examine Flora and I stood next to her, holding her hand lightly. Collias paused his work and watched as the ribbons of blue light which enveloped Flora danced around me.

"Definitely looks like she knows you," he commented.

"This is so weird. I can't believe that I lived my life and never knew magic existed. It's amazing."

Collias stopped his examination. "Are you telling me that

not only were you kidnapped, but you didn't know about paranormals?"

I couldn't believe I'd screwed up like that. "You can't tell anyone."

"For the love of..." The doctor shook his head. "I can't believe how many laws those women have broken. If anyone finds out, there will be hell to pay."

"They told me. I just...I've had a really rough day and I don't think I'm coping very well. I almost fainted when I saw you."

"So, I was the first centaur you'd seen?"

"You were the first anything I've seen. I'd only been told about witches a few minutes before you walked through the door."

"Huh."

"Huh, what?"

"You held it together really well. If someone had told me I would have taken on my human form."

"You have a human form?"

Collias laughed. "Of course, I have. How did you think I became a doctor? I can't think of any medical school that has started accepting centaurs, no matter how progressive they may be."

"So, you can change what you are, like a werewolf?" I paused a moment. "Do werewolves exist? I haven't asked that question yet."

"Yes, werewolves exist, and no, centaurs are nothing like them. A werewolf is either a human or a wolf. My natural form is what you see now, half human, half horse. When necessary, I can take either of those forms fully, for a short period of time. When I'm outside a paranormal community I take the human form."

"Is it painful?"

"It isn't me." The doctor gave a thoughtful look. "It's like wearing shoes that are a couple of sizes too small. You can do it, but it isn't that comfortable."

"I have a lot to learn, don't I?"

Dr Collias nodded. "If you're planning on staying here for any length of time, you better do it quick. If anyone outside of this house learns that you were brought here against your will, and without prior knowledge of paranormal communities, the consequences for those women out there could be dire."

"How bad?" I wouldn't say I was growing fond of them, but I didn't necessarily want to see them punished. I could see that their hearts had been in the right place. They had made a bad impulse decision for a good reason. It was just my unfortunate luck to be the victim of that impulse.

"Really bad. They could even have their magic bound."

"What is that?"

"For a witch, having their magic bound means being subject to a spell that stops any magic you try to perform from working. Any born abilities are muted as well, although they can't be taken away entirely."

I swallowed nervously. "That sounds bad."

Collias nodded. "You have no idea."

He continued his examination. "I can't see anything to warrant the fact she's unconscious. She does have some response to external stimuli, so that is a hopeful sign, and the fact that her aura is responding to you is also positive." He sighed. "I'd really prefer to get her down to the clinic so I can have a proper look at her brain activity."

"I don't think they're going to be too fond of that idea," I said.

"It'll cause a lot of questions to be asked and politically it could by dynamite. Also, this is not a natural coma. It has every indication of being a spell or a potion, which means either she did it to herself or, more likely, somebody did it to her. Either way, we take her down to the clinic and she becomes vulnerable. We can't control that."

"So, that means we leave her here."

"She'll be safer with the coven protecting her."

"Do you really think she's in that much danger?"

Collias snapped shut his medical bag and looked over at me. By this time the ribbons of Flora's aura were moving all over my body. "Witchcraft is generally a force for good. To actually harm someone magically is a path most witches won't go down. To go after the leader of a coven is uncharted territory in Walker Bay. Something is happening here, and I have a feeling that it's going to affect all of us."

We walked out of the house to find the four women talking between themselves, the tension obvious.

"How is she?" asked Isobel, the impatience pouring off her.

"From what I can tell, physically she is fine," replied Collias. "I think you're right. It is magic based, but it doesn't seem to have damaged her heart or lungs, so we don't need medical intervention immediately." He paused for a moment. "You said you were going to try a healing spell to bring her out of it."

The women nodded.

Collias sighed and crossed his arms. "I don't think it will work."

"And when did you start studying witchcraft?" asked Margot, barely containing her sarcasm.

"A healing spell is for the sick. Flora isn't sick, she's trapped."

"What are you talking about?"

"Her condition isn't because of a sleeping potion. It's because of a spell. From what I could tell, all her responses are in line with a conscious person. From a medical point of view, she should be out here screaming at you lot for doing something so stupid as kidnapping her niece. Her brain is fine, but somebody has locked down her body as effectively as if she was in chains. A healing spell is not going to fix that. You need to find whoever did this and get them to reverse the spell, or find a way to break it."

He turned to me and passed me a card with his details on it. "You need anything, for Flora or yourself, do not hesitate to contact me."

I nodded mutely and watched as he walked away.

7

"*S*he's been cursed," muttered Margot.

"Don't be ridiculous," snapped Isobel. "Nobody would curse Flora.

"If Flora's been cursed," Maude started slowly, completely ignoring Isobel, "Our timeline may have just changed. We thought the next full moon would be the best time for a healing spell, but breaking curses is a whole other story."

"How hard is it to break a curse?" Two days ago, I would never have imagined asking that kind of a question.

Believe it or not, curses are pretty rare." Tilda dragged her hand through her curly red hair. "Despite what popular culture might have you believe, witches don't throw curses around. Doing something like that requires you to sacrifice a piece of your soul. Most people aren't willing to do that. The problem is, the longer a curse goes for, the harder it is to break. The whole coven will be needed."

"So, who would be the curse breaking expert?"

The four women looked at each other. "There is no such thing as a curse breaking expert," said Maude. She lifted her eyes to the house "The strongest witch in our coven is Flora, and she would not be able to begin to break even a simple curse, let alone whatever this is."

That was not useful. I scrubbed my hands through my hair. I couldn't think anymore. I was tired, sore and I still hadn't had anything to eat. Any moment now I was going to pass out from hunger alone.

"I need to get back inside to Flora. I don't like her being alone." Isobel strode back into the house.

At least one of us knew what they had to do. As of this moment, I had no idea what I was doing, or what the next step should be. I was reacting to the situation around me, but I hadn't had much of a chance to really understand it.

"How are you going?" Tilda asked tentatively.

"I think I'm done for the day. I don't know how to help her."

"You seem to be getting upset," commented Maude.

I was stunned. "Of course, I'm upset. That woman is trapped in some magical prison, and none of you seem to be able to tell me how to fix it, despite the fact that you kidnapped me because you had some misguided belief that I would be able to do just that." My voice rose until I was almost shouting.

The three women were staring at me as if they couldn't understand why I was having a meltdown. It seemed perfectly logical to me.

Margot turned to Tilda. "I think you need to feed her."

Finally, somebody was understanding my problem. "Maybe we should also do some research into curses," I suggested.

"That would be easy if books on curses weren't banned," said Tilda.

"What are you saying?"

Maude sighed. "What she's saying is that there are no

books on curses in Walker Bay. Even showing interest in curses is a binding offense."

"As in magic binding." I remembered what Collias had told me.

Margot whistled. "Look who's learning fast."

"I wasn't really given a choice now, was I?" I said sharply.

Maude put her hands up. It looked like everyone was beginning to get concerned about my attitude. "You're going to stay with Tilda tonight, and tomorrow we'll start looking at what our options are."

It looked like my kidnappers were now desperate to get rid of me.

As I followed Tilda into her house, I couldn't stop thinking about all I had learned today.

"You're going to need to shut down your brain at some point. It isn't going to help anyone today," Tilda said as she threw her keys on the table.

I was going to answer her with my new-found attitude, but then I got a good look at the house I had stepped into. It was completely filled with plants. There were dozens of small pots overflowing with greenery scattered around the rooms. Ivy was actually climbing up the walls on the inside of the building. I couldn't say a word. I had never seen interior decorating choices like this before in my life.

"Yeah, I know. My place is unique." It seemed Tilda was expecting criticism.

"I like it," I protested. "It's almost like the house is alive."

Tilda glanced over at the kitchen, and I smiled when I saw the kitchen bench was covered in more plants.

"I was working on herbal remedies earlier today that we could use in the healing spell for Flora," she said apologetically. "Then Grandma called me, and I found out about what she did with you. I just ran out and left everything as it was." She smiled apologetically. "Would you be okay if we go to the diner for something to eat? I don't think my kitchen is suitable for cooking. Some of those plants can have unpleasant side effects if they contaminate food. I'm going to need to sterilize the whole kitchen before I can cook in there again."

"Sure," I said. "But, if we're going out, is there any way I can have a shower, and maybe borrow a change of clothes."

"Of course," Tilda said, leading me to the small bathroom.

Once again, I found myself competing for space with multiple plants.

Tilda smiled apologetically. "I like having plants with me at all times. It makes me feel calmer. I couldn't live without them."

"Trust me, this isn't even close to the weirdest thing I'm dealing with today."

"I guess not."

BY THE TIME we got to the diner I was feeling almost human again. I shouldn't have been surprised that it looked like every other diner in every small town. Tilda kept trying to tell me that Walker Bay was perfectly normal. She grabbed a couple of menus from the counter and ushered me to a booth. Sitting down, I leaned my head back against the worn vinyl. I finally felt like I could breathe. Despite the various people and creatures I was seeing walking around the town, this felt normal to me.

"What...?"

Tilda put her hand up to stop me talking and her other hand in her pocket. She pulled out a smooth stone and placed it in the middle of the table. Closing her eyes, she touched the stone and muttered some words under her breath. I looked around, sure somebody was going to be pointing at the strange woman in our booth.

"Okay, we're good. You can talk now."

"What is that?" I asked, pointing to the stone.

"That is a charm stone. A spell is put into the stone so that it can be used at a later time. That charm stone in particular provides privacy in a public place." Tilda looked around. "It means nobody can hear what we are saying."

"That sounds cool. You just carry that around with you?"

"Not all the time," Tilda said as she looked at the menu. "I just figured, considering our situation, that it might be smart."

"And by situation I assume you're talking about not wanting anyone to overhear the kidnapping victim."

Tilda smiled slightly. "That would be right."

"Is rampant eavesdropping a huge problem in this town," I asked, curiosity getting the better of me.

"Let's just say that a lot of the people around here have enhanced senses, and aren't afraid to use them."

A waitress stepped up to the booth. "Hi, Tilda. What will it be today?"

"I'll have a burger with fries, Annie."

The waitress turned towards me. "And what would you like?

"I'll have the chicken salad sandwich."

Tilda smiled as the waitress walked away. "You really wanted that chicken salad sandwich, didn't you?"

"Been thinking about it all day. How was she able to talk to us if that spell stone was working?"

Tilda tapped the stone. "It works like a bubble. Annie stepped into the bubble and we were all able to communicate with each other. The second she stepped out of the bubble she couldn't hear us anymore."

I stared at the spot Annie had been standing. "Does she know when she goes through it."

"If you're asking if it hurts, it doesn't. If you're asking if she knew, the answer is yes. Annie's seen enough of these stones that she knows exactly what it is. It also means she knows pretty much how close she needs to be to us so we are able to talk to each other."

The food arrived quickly, and I found that nothing had ever tasted so good. I couldn't tell how much of that was due to the quality of the meal and how much was due to the fact the last meal I clearly remembered eating was almost two days ago.

"You might want to slow down there," Tilda said worriedly. "The last thing we want is for you to get sick."

I swallowed and put the uneaten portion of the sandwich back on my plate. "You're probably right." I went to take a drink and then choked when a man in uniform stepped up to our table.

"Tilda," he said as he tapped the brim of his hat.

"Sheriff Tolan," Tilda replied, her voice a couple of octaves higher than it had been before.

I had to hold myself back from groaning. We didn't look suspicious at all.

The sheriff waited for a couple of seconds. "Are you going to introduce me to your friend?"

Tilda swallowed nervously. "Sure, this is Sadie Goodwin. She's just visiting for a little while."

The sheriff put out his hand. "Nice to meet you Miss Goodwin. I'm Conall Tolan, sheriff of Walker Bay."

I clasped his hand and felt the strength coursing through it. "Pleased to meet you."

His eyes stared into mine and I noticed how unusual they were, a pale blue that made me think of glaciers in the ocean. I felt my mouth go dry. I was going to assume it was from fear, although I wasn't sure what I was afraid of.

"I hope you enjoy your stay in Walker Bay, Miss Goodwin. If there's anything I can help you with, please do not hesitate to ask."

I pulled my hand back and was pleased when he relinquished it. "Thank you, Sheriff. I don't think I'll be here long, but I'll keep that in mind."

He tapped the brim of his hat again and sauntered back to the counter. Despite the fear I was feeling I had to admit that the view of him walking away was definitely one I enjoyed.

I ran a hand through my hair. "Why do I feel like I did something wrong? I'm the victim here."

"It's his gift," Tilda grumbled. "Whenever I run into him, I always feel like confessing the time I ditched school and sneaked into the movies without paying."

"Wow, you are a rebel. It's no surprise you've graduated to kidnapping."

"You're never planning on letting that go, are you?" complained Tilda.

"I think it's good for at least a few more days," I said as I started eating my dinner again.

I glanced over at the sheriff who was now sitting at the counter, staring directly at me.

"You're sure he can't hear what we're saying?" I asked.

Tilda shook her head emphatically. "Definitely not."

"Then why is he still watching me?" I muttered.

Tilda shrugged as she continued inhaling her fries. "Don't worry about it. Sheriff Tolan is suspicious of everyone. New people around here have a tendency to tweak his radar, usually not in a good way. He'll keep a close eye on you, and then someone else will roll into town and he'll move on."

"Isn't that something we should be worried about, especially considering how I came into this town." The fact that I now used the word 'we' when describing the repercussions of my kidnapping just went to show how far down this rabbit hole I had fallen.

"As long as we all keep our mouths shut, and you manage to not pass out the first time you run into a troll, we should be okay."

"What is it about trolls that you're so worried about?"

"You'll know when you see one," Tilda said sagely. "They don't come out that often so you should be fine until we've sorted the rest of this mess out."

I watched as the sheriff collected his food and headed out of the diner. "What is he?" I asked, not sure why I was curious, and wondering whether that was even an appropriate question to ask. After Dr Collias, the sheriff looked normal to me.

"Werewolf."

I stopped eating for a moment and mentally checked to see how shocked I was by that answer. After a couple of moments, I realized I was not as shocked as I thought I would be. That was a little concerning.

I asked what I thought was the next most obvious question. "Are werewolves safe to be around?"

Tilda smiled. "They're perfectly safe, unless you're a virgin."

"They sacrifice virgins?" I couldn't keep the horror out of my voice.

Tilda snorted indelicately. "No, they don't kill them. They just have that whole animal magnetism thing going for them. Werewolves are really hard to resist when they decide they want something."

I thought about that for a moment. "Doesn't it get in the way of his job, I mean the whole turning into a wolf on the full moon." I paused as I considered where I had got that knowledge from. "Do they turn into wolves on the full moon, or is that another myth I'm going to have to reevaluate?"

Tilda nodded. "They do turn into wolves on the full moon. The more powerful can control the change at other times, but the full moon is irresistible to them. The sheriff's position is usually a werewolf. They seem to excel at it. In most cases one of the non-werewolf deputies step up and becomes sheriff on the night of the full moon. That isn't necessary for Sheriff Tolan. He can't turn into a wolf, so the full moon doesn't have any power over him."

"I thought you said he was a werewolf."

"He is a werewolf. He's also the son of the werewolf clan alpha."

I waited for her to continue but she seemed to be enjoying her burger too much. "Is being a werewolf who can't turn into a wolf normal?"

Tilda shook her head. "Nobody had ever heard of it before. If you're born to werewolf parents, around the time you turn thirteen, you start going hairy on the full moon. Sheriff Tolan has four brothers that all changed as soon as they hit their teenage years. He just didn't. His parents took him to heaps of werewolf elders and healers, but nobody could tell them what was wrong with him."

"Wow, that had to be hard for him." I couldn't imagine a young boy constantly being told he was broken, through no fault of his own.

"Rumors started flying around that his mom had an affair and I think his dad might have started believing it. She left soon after, so it was just the six males all living together."

"How did he become a sheriff if he can't turn into a wolf?"

"After he graduated school, he left town. Word is that he joined the military, but that's just one of the rumor's flying around. He's never confirmed anything, and nobody is brave enough to ask. When he came back the previous sheriff recruited him as a deputy. He proved himself and when the sheriff retired, Deputy Tolan was appointed the new sheriff in Walker Bay. An election not long afterwards confirmed the appointment."

"I've got a lot to learn about this town, don't I?"

"Depends how long you plan on staying with us." Tilda finished the last of her burger. "I want you to know, we won't force you to stay here. What Grandma and Margot did today was unforgivable. I know that." She swallowed nervously. "If you want to go home, I will drive you to Augusta tomorrow, and put you on a plane back to Georgia."

I nodded, grateful that she was trying to give me a choice. "Thank you for offering that. I'll sleep on it and make my decision in the morning."

8

*A*fter the day that I had, I wasn't surprised when sleep claimed me quickly. I hoped for a dreamless night of rest to recharge so I could face the surprises that I was sure the next day would bring. I should have known that I was not going to be that lucky. Once again, I found myself in darkness, the only light that I could see came from moonlight shining through what appeared to be a window with bars on it. My brain started analyzing what was going on. This had to be a dream brought on by delayed trauma from the day I'd had. I'd never been that aware during a dreaming state, but this seemed to be a day for firsts. I figured I'd just see where it went and pull myself out of it if it got too disturbing. I shivered and was surprised that it was from the cold damp air on my skin. It was so real that a part of me believed that I had been transported into a nightmare. I felt my throat close over with fear when I heard a scrabbling noise in the darkened corner of the room. I tried to wake myself up but, despite the belief that I was in control of this situation, I couldn't wake up no matter how hard I pinched myself.

"Who is that?" I called out as I backed away from the noise, hoping that it was some harmless little rodent.

The darkness took shape and I could just make out that it might be human, although that could have been wishful thinking on my part. The shape slowly moved toward me, sliding across the floor. A face peered up at me when the light shone across it and I gasped in horror.

"Flora, what happened to you?"

Her hair was matted, and her clothes looked filthy. The smell coming from her was horrendous. If I hadn't seen this woman in bed only a few hours ago, I would have sworn she had been left in what looked like a dungeon for weeks.

"Who are you?" Flora's quavering voice sliced through my own panic.

"My name is Sadie Goodwin. Maude and Margot brought me to help you. They think we might be family." Sure, I could have gone into the whole kidnapping story, but sometimes you just have to let go of the details and stick with the big picture.

Flora shook her head as if trying to wake from a very deep sleep. "Why am I in this place? I don't remember how I got here. I just remember waking up and not being able to get out."

I squatted down next to her to bring myself to her eye level and reached a hand toward her. Part of me was curious to see if this was a dream. It had to be a dream. My hand rested on her arm. Dream or not, this felt pretty real to me.

"Flora, you're not really in here. Your body is currently lying in your bed with Isobel keeping watch over you."

"But what's happened to me?"

I licked my lips. Out of everyone who knew about this situation, I was by far the very worst person to explain it. "We think you have been cursed."

"Who?"

"No idea."

"How?"

"Not a clue."

Flora focused on me. It looked like the confusion was starting to drift away. "Do you know anything?"

"Barely more than you do."

A sharp laugh burst out of Flora and she focused on my face. "Did you say we're family?"

I shrugged. "To be perfectly honest, I have no idea. The current theory is that I am Jasper's daughter."

"Collette's son," murmured Flora.

"Yeah, the guy was barely there for my conception, so I don't have any definitive evidence, but Maude's pretty confident of her theory."

Flora reached out, put her hand over mine and closed her eyes. When she opened them again, she grimaced. "You definitely have Harstone blood running through your veins."

She didn't exactly make that sound like it was a good thing.

Flora paused as if she had started thinking again. She scrambled back out of my reach. "Did you do this to me?"

I was shocked. "You think I put a curse on you?" I threw up my hands. "Before today I didn't even know curses existed. I didn't know about witches or werewolves or centaurs. I had a nice normal life and now I've been dragged into this nightmare." I looked around the dungeon I had found myself in. "Literally."

"What did they do?"

I didn't need to ask who she was talking about. "They thought you overdosed or something, so they went looking for family members to assist with a healing spell."

Flora snorted. "I'm shocked one of you was willing to help."

"I wouldn't exactly call me willing."

Flora's head dropped. "Tell me."

I sighed. "They knocked me out and tossed me in the trunk of their car."

"Those idiots."

"Look, I'm kind of fine with it now. I can understand why they got so desperate."

Flora looked up at me. "That's pretty forgiving of you."

Maybe I was forgiving, or maybe there was something inside me that felt that it was the right thing to do, regardless of how I ended up in the middle of this situation. "I guess so." I was also beginning to think that this wasn't a dream, or at least not a normal dream. "I need to know anything you can tell me about who would want to curse you. We've got a limited amount of time to get you out of whatever this is, so anything you can tell me that will help us would be great."

Flora dropped her head and wiped her hand across her eyes. "I don't know who would curse me. I've made some unpopular decisions over the years, but a curse is a really strong reaction."

"Okay, so we don't know who put this curse on you. How do we break it?"

Flora looked at me sadly. "There is no way to break a curse. The witch who created the curse has to recant it."

That sounded like a really bad system to me.

"Why aren't there any witches who can break curses? I would think that's exactly what we need right about now."

"There used to be cursebreakers," Flora said, sadly. "Until it was decided they were too dangerous. The ability usually runs in families, and those families were wiped out centuries ago."

I was shocked at the matter-of-fact way Flora described what must have amounted to a massacre. "Why would anyone think that is a good idea?"

"For the same reason books with curses in them are

banned now. Curses are a dangerous weapon in witchcraft. The most dangerous weapon. There are still curses alive today that have lasted for thousands of years. They're the witch equivalent of a nuclear bomb. It isn't only the instant damage they cause but the devastation that can last for generations. The danger of being a cursebreaker witch was that it was so easy to fall over onto the other side of the equation. Nobody knew how to craft an impenetrable curse like a cursebreaker, and too many fell into that trap. In the end it was just considered easier to destroy both sides of that coin."

I felt sick. "That is appalling," I whispered.

Flora put a hand to her head. "Today, we look back at the atrocities of the past and hope we would never do something like that. Unfortunately, even if we were more enlightened, it's too late. The purge of cursebreakers was absolute. Not one of those families survived. The last cursebreaker was killed at least three hundred years ago."

"So, what happens to people who are cursed now?"

Flora gave me a small smile. "Nothing. Curses are so rare in the modern age that the best you can hope for is that the person who released the curse is caught and that the damage can be limited."

"No," I said, trying to project a strength that I didn't really feel. "I won't accept that. For goodness sake, I'm having a conversation with you while I'm fast asleep in my bed." I really hoped that was the case because if I had been transported here permanently, I was going to lose it. "There has got to be something else happening here, something we're all missing." I reached out and grasped Flora's hands. "Now I need you to think. Is there anyone that we can talk to who might be able to help."

Flora bowed her head. After a minute she looked up again and for the first time I saw some hope in her eyes. "About twenty years ago there was a woman called Helen Napier in our coven. She was a very talented witch. As I recall, she was married to a werewolf. My understanding is that he was having an affair." She stopped suddenly. "Never get involved with a werewolf. Monogamy isn't in their vocabulary."

"Kind of getting that message about werewolves."

"Helen found out about the affair. Rather than putting the blame where it should have gone and divorcing the cheating jerk, she decided to put a curse on the other woman."

I winced. "That seems a bit of an over-reaction."

"You would think so," Flora said softly. "Curses are not something to be played with as Helen discovered."

"What happened?"

'Flora looked sorrowful. "Helen was inexperienced, and she was driven by rage. High emotion has a tendency to mess with magic. The curse backfired and scarred Helen badly. She was expelled by the coven. What she tried to do went against everything we believe in."

"That is a horrible story. Why did you tell it to me?"

"Helen Napier is the only witch that I am aware of that has tried to create a curse since I became coven leader. We couldn't confirm it at the time, but there were rumors that her family had a grimoire that specialized in curses that had been handed down to her. It's highly illegal to own this book, but if she does have possession of it, you may be able to find information in it that could help you."

I must have looked confused.

"A grimoire is what we call a book which has magic spells or teaches magic."

I was looking forward to a time when I could have a conversation where I didn't need everything explained to me.

"So, let me get this straight. The only advice you have for me is to go to a witch who was tossed out of your coven for breaking the rules, has had twenty years to let that bitterness grow, and beg to look at a book that it is illegal for her to own. Oh, and hope she hasn't got any better at throwing curses in the last twenty years."

Flora waved her hand weakly in the air. "It sounds so much more difficult when you put it like that."

"Okay, if I get out of here I'll go talk to Helen Napier. Is there anything I can say to her that will make her feel more sympathetic to your cause?"

"Not really. Even though the decision to outcast her comes from the whole coven, I am the one who is ultimately responsible."

"Was her magic bound at least, or do I need to worry about getting turned into a toad?"

"Of course, we bound her magic. We have zero tolerance for witches who use curses."

I started to feel a strange tugging sensation. "Something's happening." I looked into her eyes, hoping this was real and that she was listening to what I was saying. "I will do everything I can, but I need you to not lose hope." I could feel Flora's hand holding me tighter, as if unwilling to let me go, but the feeling that I was fading away grew stronger.

"Whatever you do, don't give up. We will find something to help you."

9

J sat up in bed, my hand reaching out, as if it was still clasped in Flora's. All I found was the darkness in my room. For a moment I thought it must have been a dream, but then I realized that I could still feel the cold damp of the dungeon on my skin. I threw on some clothes and headed outside the house. Only then did the stench from the dungeon that seemed to be clinging to me start to dissipate. The sun was just beginning to rise, and I knew I couldn't go back inside. Even the thought of stepping back over that threshold made my throat close over in fear. I needed space around me. I blindly started walking away from the house, heading towards where the sun was rising over the horizon.

Despite my reservations about the residents of Walker Bay, I had to admit, in the early dawn, the area was beautiful. Light and shadows seemed to dance over the town, and you could truly believe that this was a magical place. I felt like I was drawn to a park which looked out over the bay. I found a bench and made myself comfortable, allowing the serenity of the sunrise to calm me. There was a part of me that wanted desperately to believe that my time with Flora had been a nightmare. Nothing more than the ramblings of a mind that had been pushed beyond its normal limits. Nobody would blame me for having a bad dream after everything I had gone through the day before. I wanted to believe that because the alternative was too horrific to imagine. Somebody had managed to create a curse that trapped Flora in a dungeon in her own mind. I had no idea how long she could survive like that, and what was worse, I had no idea how to get her out of it. I was so caught up in thinking about Flora that I didn't even notice that I was no longer alone until a voice broke through my thoughts.

"Excuse me, miss, are you okay?"

I jumped at the interruption and turned around. Terror clasped me around the throat, and I couldn't breathe. I thought that I had been getting a grasp on the different creatures in Walker Bay. What stood before me proved I had a long way to go before I could calmly meet new people in this town. Despite what I would consider a well-rounded education I had no idea what kind of creature he was. He towered over me, his large muscular body blotting out a good portion of my view. He had a bald head, pointed ears, and his skin was a dappled grayish color, broken by black tribal tattoos that wound down his arms. The only reason I didn't start screaming was the deputy's uniform that he was wearing. Surely I was safe if he was a deputy. Man, I hoped so, because I was frozen with fear. I was not going anywhere under my own steam.

"Are you okay, miss?" He pitched his deep voice low, but it still seemed to carry through the quiet stillness of the morning. I really looked at him then. Despite the completely foreign way that he looked to me, the one thing that struck me was his eyes. He had kind eyes. Of course, I'm sure there are plenty of women who originally thought some guy had kind eyes, only to find themselves painfully disillusioned. I really hoped I wasn't going to be one of them.

"I'm okay, just taking in the sunrise," I said, hoping that he would take me at my word and leave before I embarrassed myself by dropping to the ground and begging him not to hurt me.

He obviously didn't because he sat down next to me on the bench, keeping some distance, but still watching me with a worried expression on his face.

"Are you sure, Ma'am?" he asked. "It's just...you seem to be crying."

I wiped under my eyes and found tears on my fingers. No wonder the deputy was worried about me.

"I'm fine. I just had a bad dream and it seems to have affected me a bit more than I thought."

"A prophecy dream?" he asked, a concerned look in his eyes.

"I really hope not," I replied fervently. "I thought a walk would help, then I saw the sun coming up over the bay. I just wanted to watch the sunrise."

He waited as if expecting me to tell him more. "I'm Deputy Iversen. And you are?"

So, this was the famous Deputy Iversen who dared to pull Maude over for speeding. For some reason that made me feel safer and I started to breathe normally again.

"I've heard about you."

The deputy raised an eyebrow. "That was quick. You can't have been in town for that long or we would have already met."

"I arrived yesterday. I'm staying with Tilda Atwill."

"Aah, has Maude been complaining again? I'm not really evidence of the worst that law enforcement in Walker Bay has to offer."

I giggled. I would be forever grateful to Deputy Iversen

for giving me something to laugh about. "I figured there was another side to the story."

"There always is." He paused for a moment. "You still haven't told me your name. Is there a reason for that, or was it just an oversight?"

"Oh, I'm sorry. My name is Sadie Goodwin."

"Very nice to meet you Miss Goodwin."

"Please call me Sadie."

"And you can call me Karl." He paused as if thinking about what he had just said. "Unless I pull you over for speeding, then it's Deputy Iversen."

"I'll keep that in mind," I murmured as I turned my attention back to the sunrise that was spilling over the horizon.

"It sure is a beautiful way to start the day, isn't it, Sadie?"

"The best way."

We sat there quietly for a few minutes, and I had to marvel at the situation I found myself in. Forty-eight hours ago, I was living a normal life. This morning I was taking in a sunrise, sitting next to a creature that I had no idea what he was. This wasn't my normal anymore.

Karl broke the silence. "Do you need a ride back to Tilda's place."

"No, thank you. I'll just enjoy the view for a bit longer, and then I'll walk back."

"Very well then. I'll leave you to it." He stood up and we both looked over as we heard a car engine.

I was surprised to see the sheriff's truck pulling in beside Karl's car. Why was it that despite being a kidnapping victim, the last thing I wanted was to have a cop around? I shouldn't have been surprised that I was surrounded by them.

Sheriff Tolan came out of the truck and walked over to us. "Is there a problem here?"

"No problem, Sheriff," Deputy Iversen said. "Just saw

Sadie here taking in the view, so I thought I'd introduce myself and offer her a ride home."

"That's good to hear, Iversen, but I think I'll take Miss Goodwin home. My shift doesn't start for another half hour and I've got the time."

"Yes, Sheriff."

Deputy Iversen nodded his head at me and proceeded to walk away. Strange that I had begun to feel so comfortable with him, yet so uncomfortable with his boss.

"As I told Deputy Iversen, I'm perfectly okay here. I don't need a ride. I can walk back to Tilda's myself."

"I'm taking you home."

That sounded final and, as I thought about it, I realized that arguing with a werewolf sheriff might not be one of my brighter ideas.

"Very well," I said, tightly.

"Now would be good."

Most of my lessons about the paranormal were ones that had come from the women who kidnapped me. They had tried to give me as much information as possible to limit the mistakes I would make. Today I was learning my first lesson on my own. Sheriff Tolan was bossy and rude. I wondered whether that was because he was sheriff, or maybe it was a werewolf characteristic, or it could just have been him. Whichever of those options was true, I didn't care for that aspect of his personality.

"Very well," I muttered between gritted teeth as I followed him back to the car. It hardly seemed fair that my wish to watch a sunrise ended up with me being carted back to my kidnapper's house by the sheriff. One day this was going to make one hell of a story to tell my grandkids, right before they had me committed for losing my mind.

I had hoped the trip back to Tilda's house would be played out in silence. Nothing in my two meetings with

Sheriff Tolan had led me to believe he might be the chatty type. Obviously, I had misjudged him, or, more likely, I was being interrogated.

"So, how long have you known Tilda?"

"Not long."

"How long are you staying?"

I shrugged and paused for as long as I thought I could get away with.

"I'm not sure. This trip was a surprise. My plans haven't really been set in concrete."

"Where do you come from?"

"Georgia."

"Where in Georgia?"

"Augusta."

The sheriff stayed silent for a moment. I hoped that would be the end of it. I should have known better. "You don't sound like you're from Georgia."

I sighed. This was really not what I was prepared to deal with this early in the morning. "I've only lived in Augusta for a few months. I grew up everywhere. My mom moved us around a lot."

"Does your mom live in Georgia?"

I closed my eyes, the grief I usually kept hidden in a box in the back of my mind, swamped me. "My mom died five months ago."

Blessed silence. I guess that was one way to stop an interrogation.

"I'm sorry," Sheriff Tolan said quietly.

"So am I." I looked out my window as I blinked back some tears. I really could have used my mom's advice right about now.

As we pulled into Tilda's driveway, I had to stop myself from groaning. On the front porch stood Tilda and Maude, about to start searching for their lost kidnapping victim. If my mind hadn't been so focused on my disturbing night with Flora, I would have appreciated the expressions on their faces at the sight of me being returned to them in the sheriff's truck.

They rushed up to the truck as soon as I stepped out of it. Maude quickly put an arm around my shoulders as if comforting me. I wasn't fooled.

"Land sake's, Sadie. When Tilda couldn't find you, she panicked. I rushed straight over." At least that explained her outfit.

I swallowed nervously. "I just needed to take a walk."

I could see Sheriff Tolan watching the exchange with some interest.

"Thank you for the ride, Sheriff." I really wanted the man to leave. There was something about Sheriff Tolan that made me very nervous, and I didn't think it was the whole being a werewolf thing.

"You're welcome, Miss Goodwin." He nodded at Tilda and Maude before sauntering back to his truck.

As we watched him leave, Maude's arm fell from my shoulders. "What did you think you were doing?"

So much for the love. "I needed to get some air."

I turned around and headed inside, the two women trailing behind.

I grabbed a glass of water and sat down at the table, wondering how I was going to explain what had happened.

"I had a rough night and I had to get out of the house."

Guilt flashed across Maude's face. "You had a nightmare?"

"Of course, she had a nightmare. She's been kidnapped, anyone would be traumatized after something like that." Tilda sat down next to me and patted my hand. "We caused this, so we'll pay for any therapy you need."

"You have therapists?" I croaked, not sure if I was pleased or appalled that the paranormal community needed therapy.

"Of course we have therapists. You think it's easy being a witch? I go to a session every month, purely for maintenance purposes."

I sneaked a glance over at Maude. From the expression on her face, it looked like she was in the appalled camp.

"The thing is, I don't think it was a nightmare. It felt real, terrifyingly real." I took in a deep breath. "I was in a dark, cold room with bars on this one tiny window up high. It felt like how you would imagine the worst kind of dungeons would be." I took a sip of water, needing the fresh taste to wash away the feeling in my throat. "Flora was there. She was filthy and confused, and the smell was indescribable. She looked like she had been trapped there for weeks.

"What are you saying?" Maude had paled at the description of her friend.

"I don't think it was a nightmare. I think this curse has trapped her mind or her soul in that dungeon, and I think last night she managed to pull me in with her."

Both Maude and Tilda looked stunned, and, if I was honest with myself, really doubtful.

"It happened," I insisted.

Tilda kept patting my hand. "The last couple of days have been terrible for you, and we acknowledge our part in your trauma."

I could not believe she was trying to start my therapy now.

"Helen Napier," I blurted out.

"What did you just say?" Maude said, sharply.

"Flora said that Helen Napier was the last person in Walker Bay who had tried to curse someone, and it failed. She was outcast and her magic was bound. Flora said there was a rumor that she had a book of curses that had been handed down through the family." I was trying desperately to get them to believe me. My aunt was reaching out to me. I couldn't fail her. "How would I know about Helen Napier if I hadn't been speaking to Flora?"

Tilda was still patting my hand, but she looked confused. "Who's Helen Napier?"

I almost panicked at the question. Had I got it wrong? Did I have a nightmare and my sub-conscious made up all the details that I had completely believed?

One look at a deathly white Maude convinced me that it hadn't been a nightmare. "We need to get Margot and Isobel here." She drew in a shaky breath. "And then you need to tell us everything that happened to you last night."

*B*y the time Margot and Isobel turned up, I'd managed to have a shower and finally convince myself that I had removed the putrid dungeon scent from my skin. Tilda kept telling me there was nothing there, but I could still smell it.

Explaining in detail exactly what had happened the night before made me feel slightly better. The four women sat quietly as I concentrated on making sure that I told them every tiny detail of my trip into Flora's nightmare.

"What I want to know is why, out of all of us, Flora pulled you into this dungeon, and not one of us." That seemed to be the part of the story that was upsetting Isobel the most.

I did not have the time or inclination to deal with hurt feelings. "I don't know. Maybe it's because I'm family. She confirmed that I have Harstone blood in me."

"Should we say congratulations?" asked Tilda.

"Sure, congratulate me on the fact that my father is a coward who waltzes through women's beds without thinking of the ramifications of his actions. Or maybe we can congratulate me on my grandmother who didn't get what she felt was her due, so had a tantrum and ran away, leaving her thirteen-year-old sister to take on a burden she was too young to face. Or you could congratulate me on a family who turned their backs on one of their own and refused to help when you asked nicely, leaving me to be kidnapped. Lucky me."

"So, not congratulations," murmured Tilda.

"Sometimes it's better not knowing who family is," Margot said, showing a wisdom that I had not seen before.

I took in a shaky breath. "My family was my mom and I lost her. Nobody is going to be able to take her place and I'm not looking to make happy families with anybody else."

"It doesn't matter who Flora communicated with," Maude snapped. "The fact of the matter is that we have information now that we didn't have before."

"That's great," said Tilda. "But nobody has told me who this Helen Napier is. You all seem to know who Sadie is talking about, but I've lived here my whole life and I don't have a clue who she is."

Maude glanced thoughtfully at her granddaughter as if contemplating what to tell her. "Helen Napier had her magic bound, so she lives in the Glen."

Shock crossed Tilda's face. That couldn't be good.

"What is the Glen?" I interrupted.

"Remember what we said about the wards that surround Walker Bay causing paralyzing fear to those who don't have magic," Maude said.

I nodded. "It's why you're insisting that I have magic in me, even though there is nothing else in my life to indicate that is the case."

"Well, those wards have the same effect on somebody who has had their magic bound."

"So, this Helen Napier doesn't even live in Walker Bay anymore."

"Technically she does. There is a small pocket on the edge of the county which has had the wards removed. A small community has set themselves up there. They call it the Glen. They aren't able to come into the township, but they're still able to live in the area. That way they can remain close to friends and family."

"Like a village of the damned."

Maude nodded. "If you want to label it like that."

"Isn't that a little archaic to separate outcasts into their own community, away from the decent people?"

"Most of these people have committed crimes," Margot pointed out.

"I understand that, and I agree they need to be punished, but this woman committed her crime twenty years ago. Is there any opportunity at redemption?"

Maude sighed. "Now you're getting into politics. That's why we have Flora. She deals with the politics. Why don't we go about seeing whether there is a way to find out who created this curse and getting them to recant it. Then you can argue to your heart's content with Flora about the Glen."

Great, we had a plan. Sort of.

I noticed some non-verbal communication happening between the three older women. I had a feeling this was not going to be good.

"Tilda, you and Sadie will need to be the ones to talk to Helen."

My eyes swung to Maude. I did not like that idea at all. "Why?" I spluttered. I wanted to ask more but I couldn't seem to get the words out.

"The three of us were involved in the spell that bound Helen's magic," Maude said, sadly. "She won't speak to us, and she definitely won't help us."

"What makes you think she's going to talk to Tilda and me?"

"She seemed to be fond of Tilda when she was a baby and I'd take her to coven meetings," Maude replied.

"That was over twenty-five years ago." Tilda seemed as fond of this plan as I was. "I'm pretty sure I'm not as endearing as I was back then."

Maude ran a hand through her hair. I could see what this was doing to her. "I don't see any other choices," she said, desperation coloring her voice. "We'll go through some of the old books in the coven library and see if there's anything there that will help us."

It seemed the decision had been made. "Are you okay with this?" I asked Tilda who looked as surprised at the turn of events as I was.

Tilda shrugged and tried to give me a half smile. "Sure."

That sounded convincing.

Tilda pushed her chair back and stood up. "I think I have something that will help us."

"I've got a couple of questions," I said, focusing my attention back on Maude. "Do any of these people in the Glen have the ability to cast spells?"

"They have their magic bound so they can't put any spells on you," Maude said, the tone of her voice was encouraging.

"That's great to know. Are they able to hit us over the head with a big stick?"

"I guess," Maude replied, hesitation in her voice.

"Then this may not be as easy as you're telling us. Despite what you may think, people don't need magic to do damage to each other. All they need is will and a good amount of hate. Both things that I'm pretty sure this woman has in spades."

"If you have any other ideas, I would be thrilled to hear

them." I knew I shouldn't be arguing with Maude. She was just as frustrated by this situation as I was.

I slumped back in my chair. "You're right. Sorry, I think the last couple of days are catching up with me."

Maude sighed heavily. "No, I'm sorry. I wish I could say that we shouldn't have done what we did, but I can't."

Great. I hadn't been expecting a massive apology, but a little light remorse wouldn't have gone astray.

"I don't know how Flora was able to pull someone into that dungeon, but I do know that it could only be you. Even though I want to, I can't bring myself to regret what we did." She put a hand over mine. "But I want you to know, when this is over, I will do everything to make things right with you. Whatever it takes." She pulled back. "If that includes turning myself into the police, I'll do it. After we've broken the curse."

I nodded sharply. It was something.

Tilda came back into the room. "These will help."

She passed over what looked like a clay disk suspended on a piece of braided leather. I held it up and squinted at the tiny writing on the disk

"What is this?"

"It's a protection amulet, designed to keep the wearer safe from harm."

She placed the amulet over her head, and I followed her lead.

"Exactly what kind of harm are we talking here? Does it protect me from spells, or does it make me invulnerable, like Superman?"

"Of course not. It just helps you protect yourself."

"That doesn't sound that impressive."

"Just trust me." Tilda pointed me to the front door before turning around to look at her grandmother. "We've got this."

I just loved her confidence. Maybe she was right. We could go into the village of the damned and ask a woman who hated everything we stood for to help us with nothing to protect us except a small clay disk. What could possibly go wrong?

11

*D*espite the fact that I expected the Glen to look like something out of a horror movie, I was pleasantly surprised to see that it looked just like Walker Bay. The only thing that made it different was the houses were set back from the roads, with shrubs and trees crowding in the front yards, effectively hiding the houses from the street. It looked like the residents of the Glen valued their privacy. Maude had given us clear instructions on how to get to Helen Napier's house, and it wasn't long before we were parked in front of it.

"You ready to do this?" Tilda asked.

I swallowed nervously. "Would you think any less of me if I told you I'm terrified."

"I'm right there with you. If this wasn't the only way we could think of helping Flora, there is no way I'd be doing this."

"Do you think we're going to be able to break the curse?" I asked. "I want to believe that we can, but the feeling I had inside that dungeon was horrible. I felt trapped and I had this feeling in my throat like it was closing over. I was only in there for a short amount of time, and when I came out, I had to get some air. Even your house felt like it was closing in on me." I looked over at Tilda. "I've never felt true evil before, but I think what I felt last night was pretty close."

Tilda closed her hand over mine. "I don't know if we can break the curse, but I do know one thing. If it had happened to any one of us, Flora would do absolutely everything to save us, no matter how remote the chance. We have to do the same for her."

"You're right." With my resolve hardened I got out of Tilda's car. I could do this.

From the road we couldn't see Helen Napier's house. As we got closer to the front porch, I noticed that the plants closest to the house were wilting. Tilda's breathing rate increased, and I put a hand on her arm.

"What's wrong?"

"Something happened here. The plants are hurting."

"What does that mean?"

Tilda's gaze was swinging around me. "I don't know, they're not talking to me."

Okay. I was going to file that statement away with questions about weird things that I had no hope of understanding.

As we mounted the porch, I had a really bad feeling that only got worse when I knocked on the door and it swung open on its own. "This can't be good."

"What should we do?" whispered Tilda.

As if I should know. "Okay, we have two choices that I can see. One, we turn around and walk away, forget we were ever here and hope the others have been able to find some information on curses."

Tilda started pacing along the porch. "That seems to be the defeatist, not to mention cowardly, option. We came here for a reason. We need to speak to Helen Napier."

"Number two option is that we completely ignore our instincts which are screaming at us to get the hell out of here, and illegally enter the house to see if we can find something that will help Flora."

Tilda stopped pacing. "I think we have to go with option number two."

"I just want to point out that option number two sucks and is the one likely to result in bad things happening."

Tilda gripped her amulet. "We'll be okay. We've got these, remember."

I grabbed my own amulet. I really hoped my belief wasn't required for this thing to protect me. "I never thought I'd say this, but I really wish Margot and Isobel were with us."

"Me too," Tilda muttered.

I crept through the door with Tilda following me. What kept getting to me was how normal this house looked. Photos of landscapes were dotted on the walls. The lace curtains fluttered in the breeze. This did not look like the house of a woman who tried to cast a curse on her husband's mistress.

Tilda tapped on my shoulder and I turned my head. "Shouldn't we be calling out to her? Let her know that we're creeping through her house."

"You do it, you're the one she likes."

"When I was a baby. Everybody likes babies. That doesn't make me special."

"Fine," I muttered before raising my voice. "Miss Napier, my name is Sadie and I've got Tilda Atwill here. We're a bit worried about you because your door was open, and your plants aren't talking." Yes, I know, I was sounding exactly like the person you didn't want creeping around your house.

There was no answer.

"Maybe we should call somebody," Tilda suggested.

"Who, the sheriff? I'm sure he'd be understanding about the whole breaking and entering thing."

Tilda grimaced. "I don't like this."

"I don't like it either but we're here now." I took in a deep breath. "What if we look around for five minutes and then sit out on the porch and wait for her to come back."

I could see Tilda thinking about the suggested compromise. "That sounds good." She straightened her shoulders. "Let's get this done." She pointed towards the back of the house. "If this place is like most houses built in Walker Bay, the steps to the basement should be through the kitchen. If she's doing anything it will be in the basement."

My stomach twisted. That sounded great.

We found the steps and slowly made our way down them. Unlike every horror story I had ever imagined, we'd found a light and the whole basement lit up brightly.

There were shelves everywhere, creating a maze-like structure within the basement. Each of the shelves was stocked with jars containing items that I didn't even want to guess what was in them. Now this looked more like the house of a woman willing to curse her husband's girlfriend.

"I thought her magic was bound," I hissed.

"Maybe she was just keeping in practice, as a hobby, without her abilities." Tilda looked as confused as I felt.

We came around a set of shelves into an open area and I stopped. Tilda, still distracted by the items around us, bumped into my back.

"Why did you...?" She stopped her question as it strangled in her throat.

Neither of us made a sound as we stared at the horrific scene in front of us. The body of a woman was laid out on the ground with markings on the floor and the ceiling above us. My mind shied away from the thought that those markings looked like they'd been written in blood, the same blood that was pooled around the body. Small mounds of wax dotted the floor, indicating where candles had once surrounded the gruesome scene.

I clapped a hand over my mouth as I turned away. I could almost handle the sight, but the smell when we got close to the body was indescribable. Both Tilda and I bolted for the stairs and raced out of the front of the house, collapsing to the ground. I dragged in some clean air, doing anything to wipe away the stench of that basement. I looked over at Tilda to see she wasn't doing much better than me.

"Are you okay?" I croaked.

Tilda was holding her hair back, looking intently at the ground. "I think I'm going to throw up."

I was right there with her. In fact, I was amazed I hadn't vomited already. "Just keep taking in deep breaths," I said, gently while rubbing her back.

Tilda nodded as she concentrated on her breathing.

"Do you think that was Helen Napier, or a victim of hers?" I asked, not sure which of those options I wanted it to be.

"I don't know," Tilda said as the color started returning to her face.

"We need to call the cops." This was not going to help me get off Sheriff Tolan's radar.

Tilda groaned. "Yeah, we do." She pushed herself up to a standing position. "But first we need to get some photos."

I was stunned. "Are you out of your mind?" Of all the things I had expected her to say, that was not even close to the top of my list.

"The police won't tell us anything after we've been interviewed. Whatever happened in there has to have something to do with Flora's curse. We need to get a copy of the symbols and writings to the coven. They're the only ones who can tell us what they mean and whether they have anything to do with the curse."

She was right. I really didn't want her to be right, but she was. I dragged in as much of that sweet clean air as I could.

"Okay, let's get this done now so we can call the cops. I have a feeling we are going to have a long day."

I followed Tilda back down to the basement and concentrated on breathing shallowly, trying hard not to focus on the dead woman in the middle of the horror show.

"I think I've got everything," Tilda announced, her voice sounding nasally as she'd decided to pinch her nose shut to deal with the smell.

"Great, can we please call the cops now?"

12

*S*itting on the porch with my head between my knees, I didn't even look up when I heard the sirens. Tilda had managed to inject just the right amount of hysteria into the conversation when she had called in the dead body. Despite the calm way she had organized the photos, even going so far as to send them to her home computer and then deleting the photos in case her phone was seized, the panic in her voice had not been faked.

I only looked up when I heard heavy footsteps pounding up the garden path. I was really hoping that was the police. Sure enough, there was Sheriff Tolan and Karl, although I'm guessing he was expecting me to call him Deputy Iversen at a murder scene.

"Tilda. Miss Goodwin."

I barely looked up.

Sheriff Tolan eyed me critically. "You don't look too good."

"You won't either in about five minutes," I replied, caustically. I was barely holding on, and the one thing I wanted more than anything was to hide in bed and forget this day ever happened.

"That bad, huh?" murmured Karl.

"Worse."

Sheriff Tolan took his hat off and ran his hand through his hair. "You claim to have found a dead body. Can you show us?"

"No way in hell are we going back in there," I said with possibly a little too much force.

Tilda nodded in agreement. "She's in the basement. The stairs are towards the back of the house, in the kitchen."

The sheriff glanced at Karl who nodded, before entering the house alone.

"So, you got stuck with babysitting duty." I don't know why I felt the need to fill the silence with small talk.

Karl leaned against a post and crossed his arms. "Not so much babysitting, more making sure the suspects don't flee the scene."

I snorted. "Way to be subtle."

Tilda's head swung between the two of us. "How do you know each other?"

"We shared a romantic sunrise together," drawled Karl.

"Sitting next to each other on a bench does not constitute sharing," I said.

"Hey, it beat rounding up the geese that escaped from Mrs Evans' yard."

We heard footsteps coming from behind us and a much paler sheriff emerged from the house. "We're going to need everybody on this one. Definitely a murder." he barked.

I could have told him that.

"On it." Karl headed for the car.

Sheriff Tolan came down the porch steps and squatted in front of us, bringing himself down to our level. "Did you ladies want to tell me why you are visiting an outcast witch in the Glen."

"So, it was Helen Napier," I breathed. There went our best chance at finding someone who could help us break the curse.

The sheriff's voice was laced with suspicion. "Yes, it was, and you still haven't answered my question."

"We were doing a welfare check." I was grateful for Tilda's interruption. The sheriff had been looking at me intently, and I couldn't break away from those ice blue eyes. I wouldn't have been able to craft a believable lie if my life depended on it.

"A welfare check." Sheriff Tolan did not sound like he quite believed Tilda's explanation.

She nodded. "The coven had some concerns, and it was felt one of us should check to make sure everything was okay."

"And the coven nominated the two of you to perform this welfare check." The sheriff seemed skeptical.

"The understanding was that Helen may still have hard feelings towards the coven. Neither of us were present when she was bound. The hope was that she'd be more amenable to talking to us."

"Interesting," the sheriff drawled. "So, you came to do this welfare check, and what happened then?"

Tilda looked over at me. It looked like her brilliant creative streak had come to a screeching halt.

"We knocked on the door and we found it was open."

"And you decided to enter."

I raised an eyebrow. "Welfare check, remember. We were concerned."

"Of course, you were."

"We went inside and called out to her, but she didn't answer."

"Because she was dead."

I gritted my teeth. "We didn't know that at the time." I tried to relax my jaw which had become more and more tense. "We went down to the basement."

"See, there is where I get confused. You've established she's not at home, why would you go down to the basement?"

"It was the one place we thought she could be," Tilda jumped back in the conversation. "You know witches generally do their work in the basement."

Sheriff Tolan nodded. "I do know that, but Helen Napier was bound. She was no longer capable of practicing magic. Whatever put it into your head that she would be practicing magic in the basement."

Tilda's face went blank. It was back to me.

"We were looking everywhere. We figured we'd try the basement, and if she wasn't in there we'd wait out here on the porch until she came home."

The sheriff waited as if expecting me to continue. Tilda and I stayed silent. We were pretty sure that talking too much was going to get us in trouble.

"So, you found the body in the basement. What did you do next?"

"We bolted out here and tried very hard not to throw up," I said, deciding to keep the rest of this conversation as succinct as possible.

"Then what?"

"We called the police." I refused to look at Tilda. I didn't want the sheriff to get any hint that I was lying to him, another first for me.

"Immediately?" The sheriff sounded skeptical.

I chose my words carefully. "As soon as we had pulled ourselves together and were able to do so, we called the police." That was as close to the truth as we could get. I don't think he believed me though.

"You can go, but I may need to speak to the both of you again, so I'll require you to stay in town." He narrowed his eyes when looking at me.

I nodded. Chances were that I wasn't going anywhere until I'd helped Flora anyway.

The sheriff started up the steps but stopped at the front door.

"You're still herbal lore, aren't you, Tilda?"

Tilda nodded vigorously. "Absolutely. That's my specialty and I never stray from it."

Sheriff Tolan didn't seem to be put off by Tilda's inappropriate enthusiasm. "And you, Miss Goodwin. What is your specialty?"

I looked over at Tilda. Why did nobody tell me I was supposed to have a specialty?

"Sadie doesn't have a specialty," Tilda said, keeping her voice pitched low in an attempt to keep others from hearing. "She's a null. The coven is trying to help her ability to manifest." She shook her head sorrowfully. "I hope we can rely on your discretion. It's an unpleasant situation all around."

Sheriff Tolan cleared his throat and glanced over at me, sympathy in his eyes. "Of course. I may have some more questions for you later." He nodded stiffly, turned around and stalked back inside the house.

"What...?"

Tilda put her hand on mine and shook her head, throwing a worried glance towards the house. I nodded and followed her to the car. Once we got five minutes down the road, she turned her head. "You can talk now."

"Why couldn't I talk before?"

"Werewolf hearing. Usually it's pretty good. I don't know what the sheriff can hear, but I'd prefer to err on the side of caution. The last thing we need is him asking any more questions."

I nodded in agreement. "Why do I feel like you just told Sheriff Tolan something unsavory about me?"

"Because I did. Nulls who haven't come into their magic are looked on as disappointments to their family. If you were a guy, it's the equivalent of me announcing you were impotent."

Great. That was just great.

"Witchcraft is an acquired skill," Tilda continued. "You study to learn how to create spells and charms. However, you can't acquire the skill unless you have some innate ability." Tilda paused and I could see she was concentrating. "It's like being born with a talent for sport. You have that affinity, but unless you put in hard work and training, you'll never reach the top of your game. My specialty is herbal lore which means I have a strong understanding of plants and potions. However, I had to study for years before I could cast any other spells with any confidence. You've seen how Grandma's specialty is weather. She can control weather herself. After years of study, I can cast a spell which has some control over weather, but I can only do it as part of a group, all working together, and it won't be nearly as pretty or smooth as Grandma could do it."

"So, you're saying that I should have some natural specialty, and then learn the rest."

Tilda nodded. "All witches have an ability that usually manifests in their teenage years. That is their specialty. They build their skills up from that. We just need to find your specialty."

"After we help Flora."

"Yeah," Tilda said. "After that."

I really wish she'd said that with a little more optimism.

*T*he pessimistic mood continued when we got back to Flora's house and found Maude, Margot and Isobel elbow-deep in grimoires.

"Is she going to help?" asked Maude as we walked through the door.

Tilda and I grabbed a seat before answering.

"She's dead," Tilda stated, obviously deciding that being subtle was not the way she was playing today.

The three women stopped and stared at us, with identical disbelieving expressions, then all three spoke at once. "What...How?"

"We found her body in the basement," I said. "It looked like some kind of ritualistic murder." Not that I'd personally ever seen a ritualistic murder, or any murder for that matter.

"Are you sure?" asked Maude.

I tried to push down the feeling of nausea as the memory flashed through my mind. "We're sure."

"I took photos," volunteered Tilda. While she went looking for her laptop, I noticed the slightly green tinge to the women's faces and felt sorry for them. If just the thought was making them sick, the reality was going to ensure they never ate again.

Tilda brought back her laptop and I ensured I was seated as far away from the screen as I possibly could.

"Oh, Helen," Maude gasped as she touched the screen. She looked over at Tilda and me. "She was a sweet woman once. She loved holding you, Tilda. All she wanted was a family, but she got twisted up and all she could see was her hurt and her anger." Maude sighed and wiped her eyes. "It should never have ended like this."

Tilda tapped on the screen. "I took the photos for the symbols. I've never seen them before, and I thought you might recognize them."

Maude squinted at the screen. "I'm not familiar with them." She turned to Margot and Isobel. "How about you?"

The two women shook their heads.

"I feel like I've seen them," said Margot, "but I can't remember where."

I indicated the piles of grimoires in front of them. "Maybe in one of these?"

Margot shook her head. "No, I'd remember if I'd seen them this morning. I have a feeling that this memory is decades old."

"Whatever they mean, you can be sure that it's dark magic," Maude said, seriously.

Even with no magic knowledge, I would have been able to guess that. The symbols written in blood and the murdered witch were a dead giveaway.

"This is not working," Maude muttered. She looked up. "We can't do this alone. We need to bring in the rest of the coven."

Isobel slapped her hand on the table. "No, we can't. It will make Flora vulnerable. We had a plan. We should stick to it."

Maude stood up. "Yes, we had a plan, but that was before

we found out this was a curse. When Flora got sick, we thought it was an overdose. We were wrong about that. We made a list of family members to contact and we couldn't get any help. What we've been doing hasn't been working. We need to find information fast. You know every witch has their own grimoires. Surely in one of them, there is something that can help us." She took in a shaky breath and said what we were all thinking. "We're running out of time."

"But what if the person who did this is part of the coven," Isobel said, desperation in her voice. "We could be inviting more trouble in."

"That's a risk we're going to have to take." Maude said.

I could see that Isobel was completely against the idea and her concerns were valid. Margot watched the two women with a concerned expression on her face.

"Very well." Isobel stood up and clasped her hands. "We need to make sure one of us is with Flora at all times. I'll continue to stay by her side for now."

Maude looked over at me. "Are you okay with that?"

"Uh, sure," I stammered. I was still getting used to the ease these women accepted the belief that I was Flora's next of kin. Maybe when this was all over, I'd think about getting a paternity test.

"Excellent. Tilda, you need to let everyone know there is a meeting this evening. Attendance is compulsory."

"On it," Tilda said as she grabbed her phone.

Maude rubbed her hands together and glanced at the laptop. "We are going to need to show these symbols to everyone tonight, but these photos are a bit too…"

She waved her hands in the air as if she didn't quite have the words to describe how utterly terrible and distressing they were.

"I'm quite good with computers," I said. "Let me see what I can do with them to hide the body."

"Are you sure?"

I could tell Maude was not thrilled with the idea of me having to spend too much time looking at these images. I was with her one hundred percent, but I had already seen the worst of them. If we could save others from that horror, while still getting the information we needed, it would be worth it.

As I worked on the images, I tuned out the murmurs of the women working around me. Before I knew it a couple of hours had gone past and I felt a hand on my shoulder. I looked up and found Tilda with sympathy in her eyes.

"How's it going?"

I stretched my arms above my head and arched my back as I realized how much it was aching. "I'm done. I've probably been done for ages, but I've been tweaking the images to try to get them as clear as possible."

Tilda looked over my shoulder. "Thanks for doing that. Most of the coven wouldn't be used to something that gruesome, and the original images were pretty confronting. This will make it easier for them to focus on the symbols, rather than the fact that someone was murdered in town."

"Even with these pictures I don't think that fact is going to be lost on them," I murmured.

"Do you want something to eat?" Tilda asked suddenly. "I think we need to get out of here, just for a little while, before the meeting starts."

"Is it all set up?" I asked, stifling a yawn.

Tilda nodded. "Yes, as you can imagine we've been fielding calls from people wanting to know what was happening before everyone else."

Seems human nature was the same everywhere.

"Sure, something to eat would probably be a good idea."

Tilda raised her voice. "We're going to go eat at the diner. Anyone else want to come?"

Margot raised her head. "I'm in."

"How about you?" Tilda asked the two remaining women.

Maude and Isobel didn't even bother raising their heads as they shook them.

"We'll see you at the meeting house," Tilda said as she hustled me out of the door, Margot following close behind.

DESPITE THE FACT I had only been there once before, the diner was starting to feel comfortable to me. I was beginning to get used to the various paranormal races. I couldn't name all of them, but I was unlikely to run screaming down the street anymore. I smiled as Tilda pulled out her cone of silence stone. I know that probably wasn't what it was officially called, but it was how I was going to refer to it. Even though it seemed we had the weight of the world on our shoulders, we ate our meal in silence. It was as though we couldn't handle putting our fears into words. I didn't mind as it gave me an opportunity to simply watch Walker Bay on a normal day. It wasn't until we were finished that the conversation started again.

"How are you doing with everything?" Margot asked in what was obviously a rare burst of sympathy.

"I'm surprisingly okay," I said. "If you take away the whole paranormal aspect, this place is just like everywhere else."

"I know it might be hard to get your head around sometimes," said Tilda. "But we're just normal people. We love our families, we hang out with our friends, we drink too much coffee." She glared at Margot. "Some of us watch too many murder documentaries."

"They're educational."

Tilda shook her head vigorously. "Watching one every now and then is educational. Binge-watching them all weekend says you have issues and I am never turning my back on you."

Margot took a sip of her coffee. "Probably a good move."

"See, you have to stop saying things like that. There's a reason people see you as the odd one."

Margot raised an eyebrow. "I don't mind being the odd one. It means I'm being honest."

"No," said Tilda. "It means you scare people because they don't know what you're going to do next."

Margot opened her mouth. I was disappointed when her phone rang, and she shut it. I was kind of interested in what her response was going to be.

"Everything okay?" Tilda asked when the call finished.

Margot gave a small smile as she tucked her phone back in her purse. "Isobel wants to attend the meeting tonight, so she's asked me to watch Flora."

"I could do it," I volunteered. "There is no real need for me to go to the coven meeting."

"No," Margot said quickly. "You should attend. Maybe you'll see something we're missing." She looked over at Tilda. "Keep her quiet and don't let her do anything stupid."

Because stupid was what I would be going for in a meeting full of witches. I intended to make myself as invisible as possible.

As Margot walked out, I turned to Tilda. "Is she really as bad as you say?"

"You're the one she kidnapped. What do you think?"

She had a very good point.

14

The meeting house parking lot was packed. Cars, bikes and minivans - lots and lots of minivans.

"How many witches are in the coven?"

"At least a hundred," Tilda said as she pulled into a parking spot.

My jaw dropped. "A hundred. I thought covens were only about a dozen or so."

"Covens aren't limited in numbers. You move into an area and join a coven. It would be painful if they were limited in the numbers they could accept. Walker Bay isn't a huge town, but we've still got a decent number of witches. If you could only have a dozen in each coven, that would make a lot of small covens. It's bad enough that Walker Bay has two."

"How big is the other one?" I asked, unable to stifle my curiosity.

"They've got about forty."

"So, this one is more powerful?" I murmured.

"Yes and no," Tilda replied. "We could be more powerful if we wanted, especially politically, but Flora has always encouraged the coven to be more focused on the wellbeing of its members rather than political power. Flora has always emphasized that our true power comes from our bonds with the community and our families."

That explained the ridiculous number of minivans.

As I undid the seatbelt I turned to Tilda. "Okay, I'm going to need a quick rundown on the politics of this world before I walk in there or I'm going to say the wrong thing."

Tilda drew in a breath. "Alright. Politics in the paranormal world in five minutes or less. I can do this." Tilda cracked her neck from side to side. "There are three levels of politics. First level is the local covens. They deal with internal issues and disputes, and in some cases are part of the Town Council. Second level. All coven's answer to the Conclave. They are the equivalent of a federal body, but they cover the whole world. They only have jurisdiction over witches. They administer laws specifically attributable to witches. They make sure covens don't get out of control with power." Tilda peered around the car as if ensuring nobody could hear her. "Our coven is nice and friendly. We play well with the other paranormals in town. Flora is even on the Town Council to ensure harmony between the different races. Not all covens are like that and the Conclave keeps an eye on those things. They are also the ultimate arbiters for disputes between and within covens that can't be resolved at the local level." Tilda paused as if wondering what to say next. "Collette Harstone petitioned the Conclave to overturn Flora's appointment as coven leader."

"It obviously didn't work," I murmured.

"It would take a brave Conclave to overturn the prophecy of a Seer. That being said, I've heard rumors that it was a close decision."

"Why would it be close? I thought the Seer's word was law."

Tilda sighed. "As much as Flora shuns the politics of our

world, Collette revels in it, and I've heard she is a master at the game."

The more I heard about my family, the less impressed I was with them.

"The final level is the Assembly. They consist of representatives from all the paranormal races. They are the ultimate power in the paranormal world. They also manage relations with the human world."

"What do you mean by that?" I had a feeling I wasn't going to like the answer to that question.

"It wasn't that long ago that just the accusation of being a witch meant a brutal death," Tilda said softly. "Not many paranormals are trusting that humans would react well if they knew about us. The Assembly ensures they don't."

"I'm reacting okay."

Tilda smiled. "You're also coping quite admirably with the fact you were kidnapped. I figure you're compartmentalizing, and I don't want to be anywhere within your vicinity when it all finally hits you. I'm assuming there is a meltdown in your future of epic proportions."

She was probably right.

Tilda put her hand on my arm. "Are you ready to do this?"

"What am I going to do? I'm not supposed to do a speech or anything, am I?" I really hoped not. Speaking in public was not one of my strengths.

"No," said Tilda. "Definitely not. You need to stay in the background as much as possible. For now, we want to keep your relationship with Flora a secret. There is a possibility that not everyone in the coven broke ties with the rest of the Harstone family when they left. Finding out Collette's granddaughter is here could add another wrinkle into what is already a complicated situation."

That sounded like something I could do very well. Fortunately, the meeting hall was large enough that I was able to find an out of the way nook very quickly. Maude came and stood next to me with her hand on my shoulder as various people streamed into the hall. It didn't take me long to realize that her sole reason for being there was to ensure that my presence wasn't questioned. When it was time for the meeting to start, Tilda took her place and pulled up a chair next to mine.

Maude stood at the front of the room with Isobel a formidable presence at her side.

"We have gathered you today to bring grave news. Flora has become the victim of a curse."

Of course, the room erupted. There was no other way that the coven was going to respond calmly to that kind of news.

The noise carried on until Isobel let out an ear-splitting whistle.

When the room quietened down Maude continued. "We realize how distressing this is for everyone, but this is not the time for outrage. We will find whoever did this and exact justice after we break the curse."

Two people rose from their chairs in the center of the meeting hall. The woman looked older than any of the other people in the room, and she was supported by a younger man who looked to be in his sixties.

"Curses are unable to be broken. Every one of us knows that. There is nothing that can be done for Flora. We need to put our energy into finding who did this and stopping them from ever doing it again."

"No." Isobel's voice rang loudly through the hall. "Flora is our leader; we will not abandon her now."

Maude raised her hands. "We need to do both," she said simply. "If we can find who cast this curse, we may be able to get them to recant it. If we can find a way to break the curse, we will be able to track down whoever set it."

I peered out over the crowd. If you didn't know that they were witches, it would have looked like any town hall meeting. Regardless of their age or gender, they all had the same horrified look on their face. Some of the younger ones were determined, while the older ones seemed to have expressions of defeat on their faces.

"They don't think it can be broken, do they?"

I could see tears glittering in Tilda's eyes. "Curses are not broken. It is one of the facts of life for us. When you're young you think that there must be a way, there is no room for absolutes." She took in a shaky breath. "But the older ones know. They have experience on their side."

A wave of hopelessness swept through me. I barely knew Flora, but I could tell that what had happened to her would scar this group for a very long time.

"We believed we had a lead this morning and went to speak to Helen Napier," Maude continued. "Helen was murdered."

Another gasp ran through the crowd. I wasn't sure how much more they could take.

"There were symbols written around the body. We need help trying to determine what those symbols mean." Maude paused. "I am about to show you photos of the murder scene. We would prefer if you stayed to help, but I understand anyone wanting to leave at this stage."

There was silence in the room, and I was gratified to see that nobody left the hall. If we had any chance of doing this, we all had to work together.

Maude looked up on the screen as the first of the images was projected onto it. During the day I had managed to manipulate the photos of the murder scene enough to blur the truly horrific parts and make them more acceptable for a wider audience, but seeing it broadcast on a large screen on the wall brought back my memories of the morning. From the color of Tilda's face, I could see the same thing was happening to her.

"We have reason to believe Helen may have had some knowledge of the curse. We need to know what the symbols mean."

The noise level in the room seemed to rise as people started talking among themselves.

"Has anyone seen these symbols before?" Isobel asked, her voice reaching over the noise.

We looked at the crowd expectantly. Not one hand went up, not one voice was raised. I felt a sick knot in my stomach. I had hoped that someone would be able to at least point us in the right direction.

Maude sighed. "We need every one of you to go through your grimoires and see if you can find out what these symbols mean. We also need to know if anyone has books on curses or how to break a curse."

There was a swift intake of breath.

"It may be the only chance Flora has."

Once again, the room erupted as members of the audience stood up and surged towards Maude and Isobel. Some stalked out of the meeting hall, their shoulders held stiff in anger, while others drew together in clusters.

"What just happened?" I muttered to Tilda.

"Any books to do with curses are banned, but some people may have them as family heirlooms, passed on from generation to generation. Kind of like unregistered firearms people have because some ancestor brought it home from the war. Grandma just asked people to turn themselves in for hiding contraband in an attempt to save Flora. Now they have to decide what is more important to them."

"What do you think will happen?" I asked.

"I want someone to find something and turn it into us so we can save Flora."

I raised an eyebrow. "You really think that's a possibility?"

I didn't like the defeated look on Tilda's face. "I think people are self-interested. I wouldn't be surprised if someone has the answers but chooses not to share them because they don't want to get in trouble."

I looked over the remaining groups of people in the meeting hall and heard the arguments. At a time when everyone should be pulling together, they seemed to be tearing each other apart. Even among the paranormal it seemed that human nature held sway.

15

By the time Tilda and I got home after the coven meeting, my head was pounding. From the look on Tilda's face, I was pretty sure she had a matching headache. The meeting itself had been pretty quick. Information had been given and requests had been made. The majority of the evening had come after the witches had been asked to turn over any information they had on curses. It seems that despite what I had thought was a universal love for their coven leader, the realization that helping may open them up to serious sanctions had hit home. Some in the coven were desperate to help. Unfortunately, those were the least likely to have any of the self-incriminating information that we needed.

"Do you need anything before we turn in?" asked Tilda as she dropped her keys on the table.

I leaned back against a wall and closed my eyes. "The last couple of hours of my life back would be good."

A bark of laughter came from Tilda. "Yeah, that was fun to watch. I always thought our coven would come together in a crisis. Guess I was wrong."

"You never know, someone might come through."

Tilda slumped in a chair. "I always knew there was a possibility of contraband grimoires being out there, I mean, the rules on what kind of magic we can do are pretty harsh. It's like Prohibition. After years of drinking, trying to ban people from alcohol was always going to be a losing proposition. That's the same with witchcraft. For all of history, witches have been able to explore magic and try new things. They've written these spells down and passed them through the generations. Then, a few hundred years ago, they're told to stop and magic needs to be regulated because it's too dangerous. The original idea was good, it was to make us less of a visible target for witch hunters. I knew there'd have to be some who hid the not so squeaky-clean family grimoires, but it seemed harmless." She looked up at me. "It doesn't seem quite so harmless anymore."

Tilda looked back down and I saw a couple of tears drop into her lap. "I want Flora back. I want it to go back to what it was before there were curses and brutal murders. I want to still believe that our coven will always be there to protect each other, regardless of the personal cost."

I hurried over and put my arms around her. Her head rested on my shoulder and she started sobbing.

I muttered nonsensical words, assuring her that everything would be alright, even though I had a sick feeling it wouldn't be.

After a few minutes, Tilda slowly pulled herself together. She gave a short laugh as she wiped the tears away from her face. "And here I was worried about being around you when you had a meltdown."

"Don't worry, I'm pretty sure it's still in my future."

She leaned back against the couch. "Do you think you'll speak to Flora tonight?"

"I have no idea. I don't know how she managed to pull me

into whatever nightmare she's living in last night, and I don't know how she would go about doing it again, or even if she still has the strength."

"If she does, could you tell her we miss her and to keep fighting. We want her back."

"I'll make sure I tell her," I said, quietly.

When I finally got to bed it didn't take long for me to realize that Tilda's question had been answered. I was back in the dungeon, and this time Flora was standing beneath the window, looking up at the moonlight that was streaming through.

"Where are we?" I asked. The moon I could see here was a full one, but back in Walker Bay we were just past the new moon.

Flora shrugged, the stiffness of the movement seemed to show pain. "I have no idea. Every night has been a full moon. Maybe it's part of the curse."

"Why?"

Flora gave a small smile. "Because a witch is always strongest at the full moon. Maybe whoever did this is mocking me with the knowledge that even when I should be at my strongest, I am too weak to defend myself, let alone my coven."

Considering how unimpressed I was with her coven at the moment, I didn't think that was any great loss.

"But you're back which has to mean something," she frowned. "Unless you're a figment of my imagination sent to torment me."

I hadn't heard those words since my mom used them during my teenage years.

"I'm going to hope that you're not."

"I'm here," I assured her. "I don't know how, and I don't know why, but I'm here and you need to know we are doing everything we can to help you. I have a message from Tilda.

She wanted me to tell you to keep fighting. She's missing you terribly."

Flora smiled and I could see the moisture in her eyes. "She's a lovely girl. I always thought that if I had a daughter, I would have wanted her to be just like Tilda." She drew in her breath and seemed to refocus. "Did you speak to Helen Napier?"

I hated to destroy the hope I could see in Flora's eyes. "We found her. She's been murdered."

"What?"

"Tilda and I went to see Helen Napier this morning. She had been killed and symbols were written all over the floor and ceiling in her blood."

"What symbols?" Flora said, a desperate urgency in her voice.

I stared at her for a moment. Once again I was reminded why I was the worst person possible for her to communicate with. "I don't know. We had a coven meeting and asked everyone, but nobody knew what the symbols were."

"Can you remember what any of them look like?" she said urgently.

I thought for a moment. I had spent a good portion of the day staring at those symbols as I fixed up the images for the meeting. If I had a pen and paper, I could possibly provide a passable facsimile. However, I had been pulled into a dungeon where those facilities were not available. I looked up at the moonlight streaming through the barred window and found the spot where it hit the ground. The dungeon floor was covered in dirt, so I dropped to my knees and scraped some of the dirt together.

"What are you doing?" asked Flora, a perplexed tone in her voice.

"I'm trying to show you what we saw," I said as I scrubbed out my first attempt at drawing a symbol in the dirt.

Flora watched silently as I made several more attempts.

Finally, when I was satisfied that what I was drawing vaguely resembled what I had seen, I pointed to it. "Have you ever seen these?"

Flora studied them and shook her head. "No, I've never seen them before."

Great. I used my fist to scrub them out and tried a new set of symbols. It was only when I finished the third in this set that I heard Flora gasp.

My hand stilled. "What?"

Flora squatted down next to me. "I've seen those symbols before."

I could tell I wasn't going to like what she said next.

Flora pointed to two of the symbols I had drawn. "When written above and around a body these symbols dissipate the soul."

That did not sound good. Against my better judgment I asked the question. "What does that mean?"

"When a person dies, their soul comes free from the body, and they then have various options. Most move on to the other place."

"The other place?" I interrupted.

Flora waved her hand in the air. "Don't start. I don't know what your beliefs are, and we don't have the time for a debate on where a soul goes after death. All I know is that if someone dies a peaceful death and has no unfinished business they move on to the next place, waiting to be born again, and their existence continues through the ages." Flora took in a deep breath. "Or, the soul can stay behind on this realm."

"Like a ghost?"

"Yes. Ghosts usually occur when the person has died suddenly or violently. Some witches have the ability to communicate with these ghosts and help them find peace or justice and move on."

"And dissipating a soul?"

"Whoever did this not only killed Helen Napier's body, they also destroyed her soul. She can't move on, she can't find peace or justice for this life, and she can't find redemption in the next life. She is completely and utterly gone."

This just went up a whole new level of horrifying.

I sat down on the floor, my back against the wall. I'd stopped caring about the dirt and the damp. All I could see was the moment when Flora lost hope. "What do we do next?" I asked.

Flora looked over at me. "I have no idea."

16

Once again, I woke up with a start. I reached up and found tears running down my face. Flora's desolation as she realized what had happened to Helen Napier had sliced through me. She didn't believe she could be saved, and she was preparing herself for the end. We needed to get her out of there. Throwing my clothes on, I went out the front door. This time I tried to show some sensitivity and left a note for Tilda on the kitchen bench. After last night, the last thing I wanted her to worry about was my need to wander through the streets of Walker Bay as the sun came up. I headed straight for the bench I had found the day before. I needed peace, and over the last few days, this was the only place I'd found it. Sitting back and letting the first rays of the day dance over my skin made me feel alive and able to cope with whatever life decided to throw at me. At this moment, if someone had asked me where my happy place was, I would have said right at this spot. Here, I was safe and I felt content.

I should have been more surprised when the sheriff sat down next to me.

"This is becoming a bit of a habit for you, isn't it?"

"This is only my second day out here," I bit off, annoyed that my happy place had been invaded by the law.

"Habits have to start somewhere," Sheriff Tolan said as he took off his hat and placed it on the seat next to him. "Although I can see why you like this." He peered out across the bay. "Kind of peaceful, isn't it?"

"It was," I muttered.

"I like it when this town is peaceful," he continued as if I hadn't spoken. "Makes my job a hell of a lot easier."

I waited. I figured there was a point he'd get to sooner or later.

"Word around town is that there was a full coven meeting last night."

"That got around quick."

"Not really, it's noticeable when you pull a hundred people away from their families for the night. I've heard a lot of them were very distressed when they got home."

I stayed silent. There was nothing I could tell him.

"Strange thing is, several of them remarked about the stranger that attended the meeting." He glanced over in my direction. "Traditionally, coven meetings are top secret. Nobody outside of coven members are ever allowed to attend. But the word is that you were sitting in the background, listening to everything and not saying a word. Rumors are flying around town as to who you are, but nobody has any real idea."

"I'm a friend of Tilda's." I needed to stick to the party line, even though I knew he didn't believe a word I was saying.

"Maybe, but I don't think that is your only reason for being here. Things have got strange since you came into town."

I glanced over my shoulder as I heard a car pull up and breathed a bit easier when I saw it was Tilda. Standing up, I brushed down my jeans and really looked at Sheriff Tolan.

He looked tired and drawn, as if he hadn't slept in a couple of days. I was betting he hadn't.

"Believe me when I say that there was something happening in this town long before I arrived."

As I went to walk away, his hand grabbed my arm. I looked down at it and then looked up, only to be captured by those pale eyes.

"Just tell me you had nothing to do with Helen Napier's death."

I was trapped in his gaze and I could feel that hand burning through the sleeve of my jacket. "I swear, I did not have anything to do with her death. I don't know who did it. I wish I did. Maybe I'd be sleeping better at night."

Sheriff Tolan searched my eyes as if he was peering into my soul. Maybe he was. Whatever he was looking for he must have found it. He let go of my arm suddenly. "Be careful, Miss Goodwin. There is something very bad happening in Walker Bay. I would hate for you to get caught up in it."

I nodded once and turned to walk away. I may not know who killed Helen Napier, but I was already smack bang in the middle of this mess, and I couldn't see any way out of it.

"You're spending a bit more time with the sheriff than I was expecting."

I was surprised that Tilda had waited until we were back at her house before grilling me about my company for the morning.

"He wanted to know about the coven meeting last night. He's also suspicious about what I'm doing in town."

Tilda groaned. "The last thing we need is Conall Tolan looking into this."

"I know that." I couldn't help rolling my eyes. "I didn't tell him anything."

"That won't make a bit of difference. He'll find out. We need to put a plan in place to manage him when he does."

"What makes you think he'll find out. He's more focused on the murder. That will keep him busy."

"Conall was in school a few years ahead of me, so I don't know him that well, but I knew his reputation."

"What kind of reputation?" There was a part of me that really didn't want to know. And yet, the curious part won.

"Conall was the only werewolf in town who couldn't actually change into a wolf. It's pretty unheard of so that made him an oddity. On top of that, his dad is the alpha of the clan. As was his grandfather. One of his brothers will probably end up being the next alpha. And he was considered the defective runt of the litter. Could you imagine the childhood that he had?" She shook her head. "Werewolves are not the sensitive type."

"Bad?"

"I would say it's a good bet that it wasn't pleasant. A lot of people would have folded under that kind of pressure, but he stood tall and fought back, no matter who he was up against. Even outnumbered, he still put up a fight. It's how he became sheriff. Everyone knows that Conall Tolan does not bend, and he will continue to fight even when everyone thinks it's a lost cause."

"Why don't we just tell him what's going on? Seems like we could use someone like that."

Tilda shrugged. "To be honest, I don't know. With Flora unable to fulfill her duties, leadership of the coven falls to Grandma, Margot and Isobel. They made the decision not to make this official. I'm still unsure why they chose that course of action, but I don't get a say."

I considered what she said. "I think he could help. It's unlikely that Helen Napier's murder is not connected with what happened to Flora."

"It might not be," Tilda interrupted. "We don't have many murders in Walker Bay, but it has been known to happen."

"Do you really believe that?"

Tilda shook her head. "I really want to believe that."

"I spoke to Flora again last night," I said quietly.

"Is she doing okay?"

I looked down at my clasped hands. "I told her about Helen Napier, and it seemed to break her. It felt like she was giving up. I think she's preparing herself for death."

Tilda slumped down on the couch. "Did she say anything else?"

"Yeah, she recognized a couple of the symbols. She said they caused dissipation of the soul."

I was going to explain what Flora told me, but when I saw the horror on Tilda's face, I realized it wasn't necessary.

"Someone powerful is behind this," she said quietly.

"And evil," I added. "I'm pretty sure destroying a person's afterlife as well as killing them constitutes evil."

$\mathcal{I}$t was a quiet group that sat around Flora's kitchen table after I related what she had told me.

"A dissipation of the soul spell," Maude whispered, shaking her head. "What kind of person could do something like that?"

I was guessing a really, really bad one.

Maude looked over at me. "Did she say anything else?"

I shook my head. Tilda and I had discussed what we would tell the three women on our way over to Flora's house. It was one thing to tell her that Flora was giving up. It was completely another to tell Flora's closest friends. They were already dealing with everything else, I couldn't unload that on them as well. As far as I could tell, the only thing we had going for us was hope.

"We need to hit the library hard," Maude muttered. "There has got to be something in there that can help us in some way."

"You know that's unlikely." Isobel said.

"Why?" I asked. "I would have thought that the best place

to find information about this kind of magic would have been in the library."

"The coven library only contains approved grimoires," Isobel informed me.

"What does that mean?"

"Any and all grimoires which contained dark magic were burned."

I couldn't help the frown on my face. "Burned, as in destroyed, with no copies."

Maude nodded.

"Why?" I realized that I was asking that a lot, but I was having trouble understanding the politics behind some of these decisions.

"Over the last few hundred years the Conclave has worked hard to banish all magic that is harmful. Part of that was an order that all grimoires that contained questionable magic practices were destroyed. Flora complied with the Conclave edict."

"Please tell me that the Conclave kept some copies of these books for when situations like this occurred."

From the glum looks on the faces of the four women in front of me, I could see that they hadn't.

Maude put a hand up to stop my obvious tirade about a situation that I clearly knew nothing about.

"The last thousand years have seen great turmoil in the paranormal community. Very bad things happened while various beings tried to gain power, not only over our world, but the normal world as well. We've spent several hundred years trying to ensure that situation never happens again. The final act was the Purge of Spells almost forty years ago. The idea was that if the grimoires were destroyed, nobody could use that kind of magic again."

While a part of me understood what the Conclave had

been trying to achieve, the librarian in me was horrified at the destruction of knowledge they were describing.

"So, all the books were destroyed."

The women nodded.

"And now we're in the situation where the only person who could possibly help us is the psychopath who murders people and kills their souls."

"We're hoping there's somebody else that would have that knowledge. I've been talking to some of the older members of the coven to see if they remember anything," Maude said.

"Will they be willing to help if that could bring them consequences with the Conclave?" I asked.

Maude looked pained. "I'm trying to let them know that any help provided will be unlikely to be reported."

Great, that meant not only were we going up against dark magic, we were also battling people's self-interest. Never a good position to be in.

"What do you want me to do?"

"You and Tilda will go to the library with Isobel and Margot."

"No," Isobel said firmly.

Maude glanced up at the ceiling, the frustration rolling off her in waves. "Why not?"

"The library is sacred ground," insisted Isobel. "You cannot be thinking of allowing access to someone from outside the coven. It's bad enough that Tilda is entering before she's ready. An outsider is beyond the pale."

Maude slammed her hands down on the table. "Sadie is Flora's family. We may have known our coven leader for her entire life, but she is choosing to communicate with her niece. We do not have the time to second guess her choice." She drew in a breath. "We also don't have time for petty squabbles. Decisions have to be made or we are going to lose her."

I could tell Isobel wanted to continue the argument, but after a quick look at her sister, she decided to hold her tongue.

"Very well."

"I'll stay with Flora and go through these books to see if there is anything that could help us." Maude sighed. "I'll also try talking to some of the coven members again, see if they're willing to give up any more of their family secrets."

I got up from the table. "I want to see Flora before I go." I strode over to the bedroom before anyone could voice an objection.

The aura that surrounded Flora cast an eerie glow in the room. I stood over her, my hand resting lightly on her arm. Once again, the tendrils from the blue light that surrounded Flora reached out for me. Unlike the first time, their movements seemed jerky until they reached my skin and then they smoothed out.

"What's happening?" I whispered to myself and was surprised when I got an answer.

"She's getting weaker," replied Maude from the doorway, her voice cracking. "She's getting some strength from knowing that you're here. That's why the movements change when they get close to you."

"Maybe I should be the one who stays with her." Despite really wanting to do something active to help Flora, I recognized that sometimes the best thing you can do for someone is to hold their hand and just be there for them.

Maude put her hand on my arm. "The fact that you can communicate with her means any information you see can be sent to her more easily. If you hadn't been able to show her the symbols you saw last night, we would be even further behind than we are now. I know it doesn't seem like it, but the only thing going right for her is you helping us."

I smoothed Flora's gray hair from her brow and leaned

down to whisper in her ear. "We're not giving up on you. Don't you dare give up on us."

As I went to walk out of the room, Maude pulled me aside. "The sheriff has been asking about you."

"I figured he would be," I said. "I haven't told him anything."

"We may have a problem there. In his quest to find out what happened to Helen, he could put himself and us in serious danger. We may have no choice but to tell him the truth."

I thought about that. "He needs to know. If he doesn't, then we're just going to keep tripping over each other. I don't think he really believes I'm involved in Helen Napier's death, but I'm a distraction and he's wasting valuable time investigating me." The smile I gave her lacked any real humor. "And if he manages to find our killer, it makes our job just that little bit easier, doesn't it?"

"I'll think about it." Maude glanced at the kitchen. "I don't think Margot and Isobel will agree."

"Do you need them to?" I asked. From the display I'd seen earlier I'd begun to think that Maude was the one in charge.

Maude ran a hand over her face. "Coven rules state that if Flora is incapacitated, the three of us temporarily take up the mantle of leadership. We are equals in this matter. We were lucky Isobel acquiesced so easily. If she hadn't, the outcome could have been very different."

As if this situation wasn't difficult enough, now we had power plays to contend with.

18

"She really does not want me in this library, does she?" I said after getting in the car with Tilda. Isobel had insisted on separate cars and, at this point, I wasn't willing to argue with her.

Tilda grimaced. "It isn't anything against you so much. Isobel has been the coven librarian for pretty much her whole life. Letting a non-coven member into our library is just not done. It was bad enough that you attended the meeting last night. Isobel's a stickler for the rules, and ever since you walked into town, the rules seem to have gone out the window."

Considering I'd been kidnapped, I was pretty sure the rules went out the window before I'd been dragged into this town.

"Why did Isobel say that it was bad enough that you were being allowed into the library?"

Tilda smiled tightly. "Oh, I've never been in there. Only certain witches may enter the library. Isobel has complete control, and she requires extensive testing of a witch before they are permitted to access that information. It takes a lot of study, and I still have a way to go before I'm qualified."

I sighed as I looked out of the window and watched the buildings of Walker Bay passing by. I'd always thought that governing bodies that limited information to the masses were a bad thing. Seems I was having my world view challenged in more than one way.

I was surprised when we left the town and then turned down a dirt track that headed straight through the middle of a large overgrown forest. "I thought we were going to the library."

"We are," said Tilda.

"Wouldn't it be more useful for the library to be in the town, where the people are?"

Tilda smiled. "The public library with normal books is in town, but the coven library is different. Witch magic works best in nature. Too many buildings and the trappings of modern life can sometimes cause a distraction which can lead to unintended consequences, so the coven library is in a cave in the forest."

"Wait a minute, I just spent all morning hearing how dangerous these books can be and how burning some of them was considered an acceptable practice. Now you're telling me that the coven is fine with leaving them in a cave in the forest, completely unprotected."

"I wouldn't say they're unprotected," Tilda said with a smug smile as she parked the car next to Isobel.

I looked around as I got out of the car. "Okay, I can't see it."

Tilda pointed behind me. I saw a large timber door with words and symbols burnt into it. Isobel put her hand on the door and pushed. The symbols seemed to flare, and the heavy wooden door swung open to a massive room that looked like it had been carved out of rock. Okay, that was impressive. Tilda and I followed Isobel and Margot through the door.

"I can't believe there is such a large cave here."

Tilda grinned. "This forest is riddled with caves and they seem to hold some power. We used to have a couple of hermits who lived up in some of the smaller caves, and they swore that their magic was amplified out here."

I could believe that.

As we walked further into the cave, the first thing we saw were walls of shelves lining the two sides of the room, laden with books. They looked old and worn. I had never seen a collection quite like this. I walked along the shelves peering up at the hundreds of books, my fingers itching to touch them. They were all different sizes and shapes. Their binding varied from one book to the next. There was no mass production happening here. Each of these books looked like they had been created by hand.

"This is amazing," I gasped.

Margot laughed. "I forgot, you're a librarian, aren't you? This must be like striking the mother lode."

She wasn't wrong.

Margot handed over a large book with a mottled leather binding. "This one is from the early fifteen hundreds."

I snatched my hand back as if I'd been burnt. "Don't we need gloves or something?" I asked, desperate to touch, but unwilling to risk damaging something so extraordinary.

Margot smiled at my obvious apprehension at touching something so old. "Grimoires are different to normal books. They feed on magic, and the best source of magic for them are witches. Our touching these books doesn't degrade them, it provides them with strength."

I loved hearing the awe in her voice.

Margot and Isobel collected some books and placed them

in the center of a large wooden table that ran down the middle of the room.

"You two start with these ones," Margot said before she and Isobel headed deeper into the cave.

After a couple of hours making our way through the piles of grimoires we had been handed, I leaned over to Tilda and lowered my voice. "Why are there colored lights around some of these books?"

Tilda looked surprised. "You're seeing colored auras around the books?"

I nodded. "Some of the colors are kind of moving."

"That's really...um...weird. I've never heard of that happening before."

"Is it possible that I'm allergic to something in here? I'm starting to feel a little strange."

"Could it be epilepsy?"

That came out of left field. "What are you talking about?"

"Well, you're saying that you're seeing moving colors. Isn't that a symptom of epilepsy?" She stopped for a moment as if a thought had struck her. "It could be a brain tumor."

"I do not have a brain tumor," I hissed, wondering how things had escalated so quickly.

"Maybe if you walked around a little, got a bit of air."

That sounded like her first reasonable suggestion for the day. I stood up and headed towards the back of the library, marveling at the sheer size of the cave. I turned a corner and found a much smaller room with boxes scattered around, filled with more books. I sighed with happiness. This was always my favorite area of any library, the place where new books arrive and get sorted. I squatted down next to one of the boxes and pulled out one of the grimoires. It seemed to be a book on herbal lore that was handwritten with the most beautiful illustrations. As I started reading it, I could swear that I heard a murmuring in my ear.

"What are you doing in here?" Isobel's sharp voice broke through the murmuring.

I jumped and tried very hard not to drop the book. "I was taking a break and thought I'd have a look around."

"This area is a working area. Some of the books are delicate. We prefer they not be touched by anyone who hasn't had the correct training."

And since I'd had no training, I was going to assume that included me. I put the book back carefully and squeezed past her through the doorway. "Sorry."

Isobel dropped her head and I felt like a kid who was about to get told off by the teacher. "I know these are extraordinary circumstances," she said. "But there are rules, and we need to follow them."

"I understand and I'm really sorry."

As I made my way back to Tilda, a wave of nausea hit me and I leaned against the shelving. I felt something on my hand and looked up to see that the book I was leaning against had a dark red aura around it. I snatched my hand back and just watched as the shape that had touched me settled back on the book. Ignoring the nausea I was feeling, I pulled the book down from the shelf and took it back to Tilda, dropping it in front of her.

"I need you to tell me why this book is making me feel sick."

Tilda looked at me skeptically. "There is nothing on this book."

"Could you just please check it for me. Maybe there's something inside that I'm reacting to. All I know is I got sick and started seeing things when I got close to that book."

Tilda pulled the book towards herself and started reading. I sat patiently, trying desperately to control my roiling stomach.

Finally, she closed it and pushed it away. "I don't know

what you're seeing, but this book is about harmless household spells. I don't think you could have found a more innocent grimoire if you had tried."

"Then why do I see a dark aura around it, like it's been tainted somehow?"

Tilda threw up her hands. "I don't know. Maybe you're under stress and you're not sleeping well, maybe your head got hit a little harder than we thought when you were kidnapped, or maybe we should revisit the brain tumor theory."

I slumped in my seat and rubbed a hand over my face. "You could be right. I feel really strange. Between the night visits with Flora and the early mornings, I don't think I'm coping overly well."

"I think you need a nap."

"What are you talking about? I'm not a child."

"No, but you're acting as our only link to Flora. If you collapse, we lose that. It isn't worth the risk. I'm taking you back to the house. If we see anything that we need Flora to know about, we will bring you back."

A fresh wave of nausea hit me, and I gulped in some air. She was right. I was no good to anyone right now, and if I started to go downhill, I might not be able to contact Flora. Of all the things that were going on, the thought of Flora alone in the dark was the one that frightened me the most.

19

I had finally snapped. I know we were all waiting for it, but when it happened, it took me by surprise. I should have been expecting it. The only rational response to the past few days of my life was to have a complete meltdown. That was the only reason that I could think of to explain why I was in the forest as dusk started to fall on Walker Bay. Earlier in the afternoon, Tilda had taken me back to her place, fussed over me, and put me to bed like a child. The next part of the plan was for me to rest. That didn't work out so well. I'd tossed and turned for hours, unable to get more than a quick doze. I kept feeling like I needed to do something, but I had no idea what. Eventually, I gave up and left the house with the full intention of walking to Flora's place and continuing the hunt for a grimoire that would help us. That isn't quite where I ended up. Instead, I found myself heading towards the area of the forest that sat high above Walker Bay.

Two hours later I had reached a part of the forest that opened up into a clearing and provided a view of the entire town. My feet hurt, my head ached, and I had no idea why I had walked in this direction. Once again, my stomach was reacting to something, and I leaned over as a strange pain ripped through my abdomen, fighting the nausea that gripped me.

As I was bent over, I heard a strange sound as if someone was striding through the forest. I wanted badly to run, but an unknown force kept me rooted to the spot. Something lumbered into the clearing and a scream strangled in my throat. I thought I'd been dealing well with the different paranormal races in this town, but no amount of willpower was going to keep me calm in the face of this. It looked like a clay project that a small child had completed. Its form was misshapen, one arm larger than the other. Its face had no nose, just two indentations where the eyes should have been and an oversized clown mouth.

The creature stopped on the edge of the clearing, watching me as if determining what its next move should be. Despite my protesting body I turned to run, but I didn't have a chance. Belying its misshapen form, the creature moved quickly and was on top of me in a moment. It grabbed my arm and swung me to the ground. I felt my elbow wrench when I hit the dirt. As the creature moved towards me, I kicked out at its legs and screamed as it felt like my feet landed against pure rock. I tried to scramble away, only to have the creature come down on his knees beside me and push his hand into the center of my chest. I started wheezing as the pressure built like I was being crushed. I struggled against the creature, but it was like hitting solid rock. I heard gunshots and small particles of clay fell on my face. The shooting stopped and I blinked as I saw Karl and Sheriff Tolan appear over the creature, both of them desperately trying to pull it away from me. I gasped for breath as the hand lifted off my chest.

"Go," yelled Sheriff Tolan.

I scrambled back from the battle. Both Karl and the sheriff were trying to wrestle the creature down, but they may as well have been wrestling a mountain. With a flick, Sheriff Tolan was flung away and landed heavily against a tree. I could see Karl's muscles bunching and the strength he was using, but it was all pointless. The creature lurched and Karl went flying in the opposite direction of his boss. Before I could get away, the creature was on me again. Only this time it clamped its hands around my throat. I scratched and hit at it as my vision grew dark. As I started to believe that my last view of this world was a monster born of a child's imagination under the setting sun, another nightmare entered the fray. The hands were ripped from my throat and the creature was thrown to the side in the same way he had thrown the two lawmen. I blinked as the darkness receded and screamed, a scream that sounded like a croak. While the creature that attacked me looked like a demented clay figure from a preschool class, the monster that saved me looked like it came from the bowels of hell. It had an exaggerated musculature like a human with sharp claws at the end of its fingers. I knew the face would be visiting me in my nightmares. It was a combination between human and animal, neither holding sway. Only the tattered sheriff's uniform that it was wearing gave any indication to its identity. I glanced over at Karl, thanked the universe that he still looked the same, and crawled over to him.

He was trying to lift his head as I reached him. "Are you hurt?" he muttered urgently.

"Nothing that will stop me running away," I replied.

Karl glanced over at the battle as if he was just realizing what was going on. "What the hell...?"

"I don't know. I think that's the sheriff."

Karl was stunned, and I was right there with him. What had previously been a very one-sided match had now turned. The creature that had easily subdued all three of us was now being torn apart by the claws and teeth of the sheriff. Chunks of clay were flying through the air. It fell to its knees and I watched in horror as the sheriff ripped its head off and threw it to the ground. The body twitched and toppled over. Finally, it was still. Then the thing that defeated the creature turned its attention to us. Karl was already getting to his feet and grabbed my hand to pull me behind him. The sheriff roared and before we could move, he had grabbed Karl away from me and thrown him to the side.

"No!" I screamed, terrified that he was going to do to Karl what he did to the creature.

The sheriff turned to me and sniffed the air as he came closer. I felt like my fear was starting to choke me.

"Please, don't hurt us." I wiped away a couple of tears that had started making their way down my face. "Karl is your friend, you'll never forgive yourself if you hurt him."

The sheriff held out his arm and I froze as I felt him brush one of his claws against my cheek. He pulled it back and I saw a single tear had landed on it. He ducked his head and I was captured by the pale ice blue eyes that were so foreign yet so familiar.

I swallowed my fear and tentatively placed my hand over his. "Please, come back to us."

A couple of seconds passed where neither of us moved, and then everything happened at once. The sheriff groaned as if he were in a deep pain and then dropped to his knees, clamping on to my hand and dragging me with him. As we fell, we were surrounded by light that was so blinding I closed my eyes. Under my hand I felt heaving movements and heard cracking. When I opened my eyes, I saw that the sheriff was back, his face and body once more how they were when I first met him.

I sighed with relief and stared into his eyes. "Don't worry," I murmured. "You're safe now."

He responded by putting his hand around the nape of my neck, pulling my head down and sealing his lips to mine. I gasped in surprise and he took the opportunity to take the kiss deeper. Heat rushed through me and, for a moment, I forgot my fear and my pain and concentrated on the way his lips moved against mine. I was lost in a whirlpool of feelings, wanting to get closer, when I felt him go lax and he slumped to the ground.

"Deputy," I yelled, "Something's wrong."

In an instant, Karl was beside me. "What's happening?"

I had my hand on Sheriff Tolan's bare chest. "He's hot, really hot, but he's shivering. I think he might have a fever."

"We need to get him to the doctor." Karl looped one of the sheriff's arms over his shoulder and I copied the movement with the other arm. "The truck's not too far from here," he said as we started dragging the sheriff between us, his head slumped on my shoulder.

As we left the clearing, I looked back and shivered at the sight of the scattered remains of the clay creature that had attacked me. I had a bad feeling that things had just taken a turn for the worse.

hen we got to the truck, I clambered into the back seat and Karl passed the sheriff through, so he was stretched along the length of the seat with his head in my lap.

"Hold him still," ordered Karl. "We don't know how much damage that thing did to him. We don't want to hurt him anymore than he is already."

I held tight to Sheriff Tolan's shoulders as Karl threw the truck down the hill. I looked up and caught Karl watching me in the rear-view mirror.

He scrutinized my face. "How are you doing?"

That was the question of the hour. Nothing in my life had prepared me for what I had just faced. Not even my nightmares had prepared me for what had happened this evening.

"I don't understand what is going on. What was that thing?"

Karl frowned. "You're a witch. Surely you know what a golem is."

I chose to ignore the implied query. "How did you find me?"

"We've been following you," Karl gritted out, his knuckles clenched white against the steering wheel.

"I've been wandering for two hours with no idea where I was going. Why would you be following me?"

Karl nodded at the man whose head was settled in my lap. "The sheriff was concerned that you were going to get yourself in trouble."

"He took both of you away from a murder investigation to make sure I didn't hurt myself." That didn't sound right.

"Yeah, so next time a cop pulls you over and you decide to tell them that you pay their salary, remember this day."

I shot a glare at him. "I would never say that, and I don't do anything that warrants being pulled over."

"No, you just get attacked by a golem." Karl shook his head. "Where in the hell did a golem come from and why was it after you?"

"It wasn't after me, I just stumbled onto it."

Karl lifted his head and shot me a questioning look. "You may not have been paying attention, but I was. That thing was tossing the sheriff and me aside, but it wasn't trying to kill us. It was definitely trying to kill you."

I stayed silent as I looked down on the sheriff. Guilt flooded me. I shouldn't have gone off on my own like that. I wasn't that person. I wasn't brave or special. I was supposed to be at Tilda's home taking a nap.

Karl sighed. "Just tell me what you were doing out there."

"I don't know," I whispered.

"How can you not know?"

"I just don't. It was like something was making me do it, pushing me on."

"This is why I hate working cases with witches. There is never an easy answer."

I bowed my head and watched as one of my tears

dropped onto the sheriff's cheek. He unconsciously flinched and I hurriedly wiped it away.

It didn't take us long to reach Dr Collias' house and Karl jumped out and pounded on the front door. After a couple of seconds of discussion Karl came back to the truck.

"Okay, we're taking him into the clinic. I need you to keep his head straight as we try to make this movement as gentle as possible."

Despite our best intentions transferring him, we could hear from the groans that the sheriff was hurting. We laid him down on a bed and then retreated to the waiting room. We sat silently, neither of us wanting to ask a question that was going to reveal too much.

It didn't take long for the doctor to come out.

"I want to keep him in tonight. His body shows all the signs of a violent shift." He peered at us, the question obvious in his expression.

I looked over at Karl and he gave a short shake of his head. "We can't give you information, Doc. Not until the sheriff is up and about."

Collias sighed and then pointed at me. "You're up next."

"I'm fine," I said, automatically.

"Young lady, you look like you've had the stuffing kicked out of you. Even if I wasn't a doctor, I'd be able to tell that the last thing you are is fine. Now get into the examination room so I can do my job."

I followed him into the room and, after putting on a gown, I climbed up on the bed. Dr Collias started examining me and his eyes widened once he got a good look at my injuries.

"Do you want to tell me what happened?" he asked as he started cleaning up the scrapes which stretched down my arms, torso and legs.

I winced as I shook my head. "Not really."

Dr Collias paused and pulled my hair away from my neck, his eyes filled with concern at the bruises I was sure were developing there. "I'm sorry, but I have to ask this. I need to know if either of the men who brought you in tonight did this," he said, softly.

"No," I replied immediately. "Definitely not."

"So, I'm assuming they saved you from something."

I nodded gently.

"Good." He continued on with his work. "You know, if there's anything you need to talk to me about, I'm here."

"Thank you," I whispered.

By the time the doctor had finished with me, I looked worse than when I'd started.

"Is she okay?" asked Karl as we walked back into the waiting room.

Dr Collias nodded. "I recommend rest and giving herself time to heal, but I have a feeling that's not in anyone's future."

I could see the resignation on Karl's face as he agreed. "I'll take her to Tilda's and then I'll be back to watch over the sheriff." He eyed Collias keenly. "Can you take care of him until I return?"

"Nobody will get near my patient." With those words I no longer saw the gentle healer that he was, I saw the centaur warrior that he could be.

Before I knew it, I was bundled back in the sheriff's truck and we were heading towards Tilda's place.

"Are we going to talk about what happened?" I asked, not sure if that was something I wanted to do.

Karl sighed and rubbed a hand over his face. "I need to work some things out before we have that conversation."

I could understand that. I watched the town go by and before we knew it, we were sitting in front of Tilda's house. I was grateful to see that the building was cloaked in darkness.

"Looks like she's not home yet."

Karl leaned over and put a hand on my arm. I looked down and marveled at the fact that a few days ago the mottled gray of his hand would have seemed so alien to me. Now I felt like it was the only thing keeping me grounded.

"I need to do some research. Until I get a better handle on all this, I'd rather not speculate. I think that could get us into more trouble than we're already in."

That sounded reasonable. I went to get out of the truck when I felt Karl's hand tighten on me.

"I need to ask you to not say a word of what happened this evening to anyone."

"I don't know if I can promise that," I said. "I think the coven needs to know about the golem. There are things happening that I can't talk about, and I'm pretty sure my getting attacked by that thing is going to be pertinent to that."

"Okay," Karl said. "I can understand that. Can you at least keep what happened to the sheriff quiet?"

I nodded. "I don't see how it's relevant at this stage, I won't say a word."

"Thank you. I have a bad feeling this is going to blow up soon. I don't want the sheriff to be collateral damage."

"Neither do I," I murmured, remembering that kiss.

$\mathcal{I}$ was grateful that Tilda wasn't home yet. Unfortunately, the evening had left its mark on me, most noticeably on my throat in the form of massive bruises which caused me to wince when I saw them in the mirror. There was no way I was going to be able to hide what had happened, so I decided my best plan was to retreat to the bedroom. I didn't come out when I heard Tilda come home, and pretended to be asleep when she carefully opened the door to check on me. I just needed a bit of time to work out how I was going to explain what had happened and, most importantly, why I had felt this overwhelming need to wander through the forest.

I was no longer surprised to find myself in the dark tower with Flora sitting with her back against a wall and her head resting on her knees. If it was at all possible, she looked worse than she had the previous two nights.

"Are you getting any sleep?" I asked.

"No sleep, no food and nobody comes to visit." She gave me a rueful smile when she raised her head. "You know, I'd almost be grateful if the villain turned up to mock me at this stage. At least I'd know who the bad guy is."

I sat down next to her and mirrored her position. "Have you come up with any idea as to who did this to you?"

Flora shook her head. "I didn't think I'd done anything in my life that would warrant this kind of hate."

"When I was first brought here, the coven thought you'd been getting sick over the last couple of months. They thought something was happening with you, both mentally and physically."

Flora ran her hand through her hair, only to have it get stuck at the top of her scalp. "This is so disgusting," she sighed as she tried to disentangle her fingers.

I wasn't going to disagree.

"The last couple of months I've been feeling a bit strange, a little forgetful, just generally unwell. I saw Dr Collias and he had some tests done, but he said there was nothing physically wrong with me." She took in a shuddery breath. "I was afraid there was something happening mentally."

Things started coming together in my mind. "Is it possible that someone was doing something to you? Maybe some low-level spells or potions, not meant to kill you, just to soften you up."

Flora's eyes sparked. "In preparation for the curse."

"It's a thought. My understanding is that as coven leader you're a pretty strong witch. Maybe, whoever did this was concerned that you'd be able to fight off the curse and thought weakening you before casting it was a good way to go."

"You could be right."

"Which also means that it wouldn't be a one-off thing which could mean a stranger. If we believe they did it over a couple of months…"

"It would have to be somebody I knew and was comfortable with," Flora finished the thought.

"Yeah."

"I don't like that line of thinking," Flora said, anger sparking in her eyes.

"Look, I can understand that. I'm an outsider to this town and have no idea how it works. I'm just throwing suggestions out there so we can see what sticks." I waited for her to think about it.

"It's possible," she whispered.

"Do you have any thoughts as to who it might be?" I was trying to be gentle. This had to be hurting her.

Flora laughed bitterly. "Do I have any thoughts as to who among the people I trust and call friends would hate me so much as to trap me in this place for eternity. I have to say, I have no idea."

Okay, we needed to try a new tack. "They would have had to have easy access to you and your potion supplies."

"My home is open to everyone. Anyone could have accessed those things."

"You might want to re-think that policy when we get you out of here," I muttered.

"I think you could be right," Flora laughed, though there wasn't any humor in it.

Which brought us to a question I really did not want to ask. "The night before you ended up here, did you take a sleeping potion?"

Flora nodded. "I take some when I have trouble sleeping. The last couple of months I've had a touch of insomnia."

"There was originally a concern that you overdosed, on purpose."

Flora shook her head. "No, nobody could possibly believe that."

"I'm afraid they did. It seems there was a whole bottle of

the sleeping potion that was full the night before, and was empty the next morning."

"No, that can't be right. I remember, it was a new bottle and I only had about a teaspoon of it, well within the normal range."

"Then that means somebody got rid of the rest of the potion to make everyone believe you overdosed. A couple of months of physical illness and mental confusion played right into it. It wasn't until Dr Collias examined you that we determined that it was a curse. Without him it might have been weeks before we worked out what was wrong."

"Whoever cast the curse was in my house that night while I was asleep."

"Do you have any security?" I asked.

"No," Flora said ruefully. "Until right at this moment I never thought I needed any."

"So, it could have been anyone in Walker Bay." I couldn't keep the disappointment from my voice.

"I'm sorry I couldn't be more help," Flora said in a small voice. "I may have got complacent. I never wanted to believe that the intrigues of witch politics could strike us." She looked at me carefully. "What happened to your neck?" She pulled my hair back to examine the bruising.

"That's another thing I needed to talk to you about. I went wandering in the forest and got attacked by something called a golem."

"There's a golem in Walker Bay?" Flora's voice started to rise, and I could detect the note of panic.

"Yes, earlier this evening it tried to kill me, and I'm pretty sure I was the target. It seemed rather single-minded in getting to me."

"How did you get away from it?" Flora asked.

"I really don't think that's the important part of what happened." I wasn't going to betray Sheriff Tolan, even though Flora wasn't in a position to tell anyone else. "What I need to know is, what is a golem and why was it there?"

"Simply put, a golem is a creature that can be manufactured out of something like clay and given a semblance of life using magic spells. They are usually created to protect something of great value. They are dangerous and impossible to destroy."

I had to stop myself from correcting her on that point.

"If there is a golem running around in the forest, then there is something out there that is very important to somebody," Flora leaned forward, urgency in her voice.

"What are the chances that it is related to what happened to you?" I asked.

"Creating a golem is difficult and takes a level of magic that is comparable to a curse. The belief that we have two witches in Walker Bay who are not only capable of this kind of magic, but willing to sacrifice part of their soul to do it, is too disturbing to contemplate."

"So, in answer to my question, you're saying that I need to go back up there and find out what it is that the golem was protecting."

"I really wish I wasn't saying that," Flora said, quietly.

I wish she wasn't saying it either.

22

*O*nce again, I woke up feeling like there was a lead weight on my chest. The nights spent sitting in that cell with Flora were definitely causing some issues. The first thing I wanted when I woke up was to get away from any enclosed spaces and watch the sun flaming across the horizon. I didn't bother leaving a note as I figured by now Tilda had a good idea where to find me if she needed to. When I reached the bench and looked out across the bay I started taking in some deep breaths.

"You're going to hyperventilate," Karl noted, as he dropped beside me.

I really should work more on my spatial awareness. "Didn't expect to see you out here this early."

"I figured we needed to talk before this day starts, make sure everybody is on the same page."

"How is he?"

Karl rolled his head and I heard a couple of creaks in his neck. It looked like I wasn't the only one to have a rough night. "Well now, I don't rightly know. A couple of hours after I dropped you off, he woke up and busted out of the clinic."

"Where did he go?" I asked, the alarm filling my voice.

"I followed him back to his place."

"Was that safe?"

Karl snorted. "After last night, I wasn't going to get in his way."

"What happened last night?" I needed to know. I thought I'd been keeping a handle on things, but last night the situation had spiraled out of control. If I was going back up that hill to find out what the golem was protecting, I needed every little bit of information that I could get a hold of.

"Well," drawled Karl, "last night you got attacked by a golem and, if I'm not mistaken, my boss turned into a berserker." Karl rubbed his hand over his face. "Damn, I need a drink."

"What's a berserker?" I asked tentatively because a part of me didn't think I wanted to know.

Karl gave me a sharp look. "Berserkers are from myths. Famous warrior werewolves with a lot of crazy in them. I don't know much about them, but there hasn't been one on record since the Middle Ages. They're considered dangerous and unstable."

"And the sheriff is one of these?"

"That's my best guess."

"That's going to be a problem, isn't it?"

"And there is the understatement of the day." Karl looked over at me and I squirmed under his assessing gaze. "Now I have a question for you."

I had a feeling I wasn't going to like this.

"Can you tell me why you had no idea what a golem was."

"I know what a golem is," I said defensively.

"You may know what one is now, but I will bet a good

portion of my salary that last night you didn't have the faintest clue what one was."

I stayed silent, chewing on my lower lip.

Karl sighed. "There's something about you that doesn't quite fit. You realize that, don't you?"

"I'm sorry," I whispered. "I just can't give you the answers you're looking for right now."

"Is there a possibility I'll get them in the future?" he asked, his eyes studying me closely.

I shrugged. Once again, he was asking questions of the wrong person.

Karl sighed and leaned back against the bench. "Fair warning, usually the coven is given a fairly long leash because the witch laws are so much stricter than normal laws." He paused, obviously looking for the best way to frame what was coming. "That isn't going to last. Things are happening in town, and I have a feeling that the coven is smack bang in the middle of it."

"I understand," I murmured.

"I'm glad you do because I thought I had a handle on everything that happens in this town, but as of yesterday I've realized that I know nothing."

We fell silent for a few minutes, having reached an impasse and unsure how to proceed.

"Can I ask you a question about last night?" I asked, feeling my face go red.

Karl glanced over at me and for the first time this morning I saw a small grin on his face. "From the amount of blushing you've got going on, I'm assuming you want to know about the kiss."

I nodded. I know, considering everything else that was happening, focusing on a kiss may seem to be a frivolous thing, but it was taking up too much of my focus for me to ignore.

"Okay, everyone knows werewolves are instinctual creatures. Their base natures have a tendency to get away from them sometimes."

"But they're also human. Shouldn't that keep them civilized?"

"You'd think so, but humans can be slaves to their baser natures as well. Hormones get involved and things have a tendency to get out of control. Trust me when I say that being a guy and going to high school with werewolves is not fun." He paused for a moment and lowered his voice, even though there was nobody around us. "Being a berserker ramps everything up. What the sheriff went through last night was intense. He could have just been reacting to it on pure instinct. Chances are he won't even remember what happened before he passed out."

That made sense. Last night had been a very surreal situation. "So, the sheriff was just acting as a werewolf. It meant nothing." I wondered why disappointment was slashing through me.

Karl put his hand on mine and squeezed. "I'm sorry if that wasn't the answer you were looking for."

I forced a smile as I looked up at him. "I don't know why it's bothering me."

"Last night wasn't just an intense situation for the sheriff. It had to be terrifying for you as well. It's no wonder your emotions are heightened."

"What the hell are you doing, Deputy?" a voice growled at us.

I blinked up at the interruption to find Sheriff Tolan glaring at us. He looked far better than last night, but he also looked like he wanted to rip off the hand Karl was very quickly removing.

"We're just talking, Sheriff."

"Finish it up. We've got work to do." Without even looking at me, the sheriff spun around and stalked off.

"Of course, there is also the distinct possibility that I have no idea what I'm talking about," muttered Karl as he hurried off after his boss.

or the first time I actually had to find my own way back to Tilda's house after my morning walk. When I strode into the kitchen I found Tilda and Maude seated around the table, talking intently.

"What the...?" Tilda glanced at her grandmother and rethought her choice of words. "What happened to you?"

I dragged myself into a chair and winced as I sat down. "Last night, I went for a walk and ended up being attacked by a golem."

Both their jaws dropped. From their reactions I was assuming that was one of the last scenarios they were expecting.

"Are you sure?" asked Tilda.

"Yeah, I'm pretty sure that a golem threw me around and then tried to strangle me."

"How did you know it was a golem?" Maude asked, suspicion coloring her tone.

"I'm a quick study."

"I'm trying very hard to believe what you're saying," Maude said with a healthy dose of skepticism. "The problem is that you're saying that a golem attacked you, but you got away."

"Yes."

"Well, unless you've got some superpowers that you have neglected to share with the rest of the group, and I am going to remind you that it was only a few days ago that you were taken down by two women slightly past their prime, it would have been impossible for you to escape from a golem."

"Something came out of the forest and created a diversion." That was as close to the truth as I was going to get. "And you know the worst thing, despite the fact I was attacked and despite the fact that I hurt on every level, I still have this aching need to go back up there." I looked over at Tilda and Maude. "That's not normal, is it?"

"Did you see Flora last night?" Maude asked with a sudden shift in the conversation.

I sobered a bit as I remembered how Flora had been and the discussion we'd had. In light of that conversation I wondered if I was being foolish trusting these women.

"How is she holding up?" asked Tilda.

"She's strong." I decided that until I had more information, our theory about someone within the coven trying to hurt her was going to stay just between me and Flora.

"Did she have anything more to say?" asked Maude shrewdly. I could tell from the way she was looking at me that she knew I was holding things back. I lifted my head and looked her square in the eyes. "She thinks I need to find out what the golem was protecting."

"Oh, that doesn't sound like a good idea."

I couldn't agree more with Tilda on that one. "I don't see any other options."

"I think you're right," said Maude as she stood up abruptly.

"You mean, now?" Tilda's whining didn't really fit with the whole witch persona.

Maude took pity on her. "You can stay here. You don't have to come."

Tilda crossed her arms and snorted. "Sure, because letting my grandmother go traipsing through the forest when there's a golem running around loose is something that I'm going to do."

Maude pulled herself up to her full height. "I have been taking care of myself far longer than you have been alive, young lady." With that she swept out of the room.

"Great," groaned Tilda. "As if today wasn't going to be a bad day already. She's going to be impossible now."

I really didn't want to get into the family dynamics. "Should we follow her?"

Tilda stood up, a resigned expression on her face. "She won't go without us. We need you to point us in the right direction. Just wait here for a minute."

"Why?"

"I'll get you another protection amulet. You should be wearing one every time you leave the house."

I touched the bruising on my throat. I had a horrible feeling that no protection amulet would have saved me.

BY THE TIME we reached the spot I had been the previous night, I was feeling slightly better. That could have partly been because I could still see the pieces of clay strewn about the clearing. I'm pretty sure there was a part of me that thought the golem might have pulled itself together during the night.

Maude shivered despite the warmth of the morning. "You can tell something evil happened here."

I looked at her curiously. "So, golems are dark magic?"

"The creation of a mindless, soulless slave who will do anything that its master tells it to do regardless of the morality of the act. You bet your sweet patootie it's dark magic." Her eyes narrowed as she focused on the pieces of clay. "That's impossible," she muttered as she stepped closer, finally stopping when she reached the head. She wrapped the scarf she was wearing around her hand and pushed the head into an upright position.

She stepped back suddenly and strode purposefully over to me, her hand grabbed my arm and held on tight.

"What's wrong?" I asked, a little frightened by the expression on her face.

"Grandma," Tilda said, the warning clear in her voice.

Maude looked up into my eyes and it felt like she was peering into my soul. "This is important, Sadie. I need you to be totally honest with me."

"Of course," I said as I prepared to lie my head off. I may not know the sheriff well, but he had saved my life. If lying protected him, then I was going to do it.

"Did you destroy this thing?"

I breathed a little easier. That question I could answer with complete honesty. "No, I swear, I did not do this."

"Then we may have more to worry about here than someone who can create a golem."

"What do you mean?"

Maude looked meaningfully at the various pieces of clay scattered around us. "Whatever destroyed this thing is dangerous."

I knew he was dangerous. I'd seen the sheriff tear this thing apart with his bare hands...and teeth. Big, scary teeth. I don't think that was all she was talking about though.

"What do you mean?"

"Physical strength wouldn't have done this alone. It

would have taken a strong kind of magic to pull apart a golem." She let go of my arm and started wandering around the clearing, touching pieces of the golem, but always making sure her hand was wrapped as if that would give her protection against the dark magic.

"She looks upset," I remarked to Tilda as we both sat on a boulder and watched the older woman kicking over pieces of clay while muttering to herself.

Tilda laughed tonelessly. "A curse on Flora, a golem running around, and then something that could kill that golem, and we have no clue what it is. I'm pretty sure this is all of Grandma's nightmares rolled into one."

"Is this kind of thing normal for Walker Bay." I was suddenly curious. "Is there usually so much...?" I waved my hand in the air.

"Drama," supplied Tilda.

"Yeah."

"Definitely not. Usually the worst thing we have to deal with is a pack of werewolves going nuts on a full moon."

Maude called Tilda over and started pointing to various things on the ground. I could tell the presence of the golem was disturbing her, only to be made worse by the fact something had managed to destroy it. She kept looking over at me. I knew she was going to start asking other questions and I was going to have to lie to her. I didn't want to do that, but I didn't have a choice. When the golem had his hands around my neck, I knew I was going to die. The sheriff saved my life. For that alone, he deserved my loyalty in this matter.

I rubbed the back of my neck and winced at the pain. I could still feel those misshapen fingers wrapped around my throat. That's when I saw it, hidden in the corner of the clearing, leading into the forest. It was like a strip of darkness that wound through the undergrowth like a pathway. I watched as the blackness twisted around on itself. My stomach clenched and I felt sweat dripping down my face. I looked over to where Tilda and Maude were having an intense whispered discussion. If I wanted to, I could slip away now and they wouldn't realize. That would be what I'd do if I was a cute co-ed who'd just made out with her boyfriend in a horror film. Fortunately, I wasn't.

"I think we need to go that way," I said, pointing towards the blackness.

Maude looked in the direction I was pointing. "Why do we need to go there?" she asked, a quizzical look on her face.

I guess that answered the question whether they were able to see what I could see. I had a feeling that if I described the soul sucking darkness that was leading deeper into the forest, that I would have a whole new set of problems. It seemed everyone in this town played things close to the vest. I was going to stick with that.

"The golem came from that direction last night when it came out of the forest."

That sounded reasonable to me, although Maude looked slightly skeptical. Of course, her world view had been thrown off course over the last few days.

"Are you sure?"

I wasn't even close to sure, but that feeling inside of me that had compelled me to climb up to this clearing the night before was now telling me that I had to follow the darkness.

"As sure as I can be," I muttered and headed for the pathway.

Maude and Tilda fell in behind me. I followed the darkness, ensuring that no part of me touched it.

"Careful," I barked at Tilda as she was about to step into the middle of it. I yanked on her arm and pulled her behind me. "Just follow in my footsteps."

"You're being really weird," Tilda said, her eyes wide.

I took a moment to appreciate the irony of that statement coming from a witch. "Just trust me, please."

The two women nodded. I was hoping they'd attribute my strange behavior to the various injuries I now sported, thanks to my unwilling expedition into the world of the paranormal, because I was not yet willing to explain any of it. The pathway opened into another small clearing and the darkness led straight into the mouth of a cave. Well, that was just great.

"Please tell me we don't have to go in there." Tilda said, her voice quavering.

If it came down to a vote, I really wanted to vote no. "If I had to guess I would say that the golem was protecting something in there." I said. "If we want to find out what it was, we need to go in."

"We need a light." Trust Maude to cut right through the fear and land on the practical.

Tilda help up her phone. "I've got a light app."

I burst out laughing, I couldn't help it. Of all the surreal moments I had been through, this one topped them all. I had followed a path of darkness to a cave that had been protected by a golem with two witches at my back. This was the moment somebody was supposed to produce a flaming torch and we'd boldly go forth on our quest. The phone lighting the way just didn't seem to quite fit the scenario.

"Are you quite done?" I could tell I was pushing the limits of Maude's patience.

I wiped the tears from my eyes. "Yes, I'm good. Just had a moment there, it's over now."

Maude took the phone from Tilda. "I'll go first." She put up a hand to stop the argument she could see coming. "I may be old, but I'm still the strongest out of all of us."

Tilda and I looked at each other. Unfortunately, she wasn't wrong. We followed Maude as she carefully made her way into the darkness. As Maude swung the phone around, I could see that this cave, unlike the library one, was small with a lot of dark corners.

"Well, that's disappointing," said Tilda as she swung her eyes around the cave. "It doesn't look like there is anything here."

"Maybe we're missing something," muttered Maude as she squinted at the shadows.

I stood silently in the middle of the cave, my eyes fixed to an area where it looked like a pile of black worms were squirming over the top of what seemed to be a small wooden chest. I had to ask the question. "Do either of you see something over there?"

Tilda and Maude crowded around me. "I think I see something now that you've pointed it out. Is that a box?" Maude went to step forward.

"Wait a minute," I said as I grabbed her arm.

Maude looked pointedly at my hand and I dropped it quickly.

"Could you just take my word that we need to approach that thing carefully." I didn't want to tell them what I saw, but I also didn't want them to unknowingly touch something that could hurt them.

Maude gestured to the box and I knelt next to it. Pulling my jacket sleeve down until it covered my hand I swiped at the black tendrils until they moved away from the catch. With shaking hands, I opened the lid. I don't know what I was expecting, but it wasn't a flat rock. I could make out some scratches on it but, to be honest, I'd been hoping for a grimoire which would answer all our questions.

"It's just a rock," I said, the disappointment clear in my voice.

I heard Maude gasp and looked up to find her hand pressed against her mouth, her face drawn with fear.

"I'm thinking that things just got worse," I sighed.

Maude shook her head, her shoulders bowed as if she had taken one knock too many. "A curse tablet," she whispered. "I can't believe I'm looking at a curse tablet."

"From your reaction, I'm assuming that's bad."

"Curse tablets are the worst kind of dark magic. Their use was outlawed centuries ago."

Because this situation wasn't already as bad as it could get.

"Do you want to take it?" I asked, looking up at her.

"I can't."

I slammed the chest shut and held out my hand. "I need your scarf."

Maude handed it to me wordlessly and I wrapped it around the box. I had no idea whether that would contain the evil I could feel dripping from the piece of stone, but it made me feel better about carrying it.

"We better get this home, it could help us save Flora," I said, a rare feeling of hope surging through me..

"Or it could open up a whole new level of problems," Maude muttered, a bleak expression on her face.

I really hoped she was wrong.

*a*s I walked out of the cave, the wooden chest wrapped in Maude's scarf, I stopped suddenly and almost got knocked over by Tilda who ran into the back of me.

"Why did you...? Oh dear."

"Ladies," Sheriff Tolan drawled as he pushed himself up from the boulder he was leaning against. "What a delightful surprise to see you on this fine day."

I was going to assume he was being sarcastic.

"Now, would you like to explain why on Earth you're up here?"

Maude opened her mouth and the sheriff put his hand up.

"Before you start with whatever story you have concocted to protect coven secrets, I want you to know that I am a little on edge at the moment, and it won't take much for me to lock you all up for as long as I can find a reason to. You should be aware that I'm feeling creative today."

"You're right, Sheriff," Maude said, a resigned expression on her face. "It's time that we told you everything. If you'll follow us back to Tilda's house..."

The sheriff shook his head. "No, I think we've gone past the point where the coven dictates our terms of engagement. We'll be going down to my office and having our discussion there."

I could see Maude wanted to argue with him. I wanted to argue with him, but one look at the sheriff's determined expression put paid to that.

"Very well, Sheriff Tolan," Maude replied in a way that managed to be both accepting yet hinted at future retribution.

The sheriff gestured towards the pathway. "After you."

"When we got back to the vehicles, Maude threw her keys at Tilda. "You're driving."

"Great," Tilda muttered.

"And I'll be driving behind you so watch your speed," called out Sheriff Tolan.

"Just great."

Maude pushed me into the back seat of the car and followed me in. "Buckle up, we need to get Margot and Isobel on this. There's no telling how long that boy is going to keep us tied up." She looked down at the box which I'd settled between us. No way was I having that thing sitting in my lap. "I'm going to need you to open it up."

I covered up my hands again and opened the box. Maude peered in and took a couple of photos. She concentrated on her phone and her fingers started flying. I figured now wasn't the right time to express how impressed I was at her texting ability.

Once she was finished, she put her phone away and gestured at the box. "You can close it now. I really don't want to look at that thing any more than I have to."

I closed the lid and wrapped the scarf securely over it. "So, are you going to tell me what a curse tablet is?"

Maude sighed and pulled her attention back to me. "A

curse is bad enough, but if it's embodied in a tablet it lasts as long as the tablet does. There are still curse tablets being found in ruins from thousands of years ago."

"So, it's worse than we thought."

"Somewhere out there we have a witch who is practicing magic so dark that they must have forfeited their entire soul to do it."

"Why would they do that?" I asked. "I know this sounds harsh, but wouldn't it have been easier to just kill her?"

"It would have been easier, but I don't think this is about killing Flora. This is a statement. To create a curse tablet and a golem to protect it, all of which is going against everything the Conclave has been trying to institute for the last several hundred years, this doesn't sound like a personal grudge. There is something much deeper happening here. We may have to bring the Conclave in on it."

From the look I could see on Tilda's face in the rear-view mirror, that was not the most popular option.

When we pulled up at the sheriff's office Maude put her hand on my arm. "Let me do the talking."

I was completely fine with that. "What did you want me to do with the box?"

Maude stilled. "There's no way we can leave it in the car, it's too dangerous. You'll need to bring it in with you."

"You don't think that the sheriff is going to object to me lugging this thing through his office. For all he knows it could be a weapon."

"It is a weapon," Maude replied. "And we're going to be explaining what we were doing up in that cave anyway. We may as well make it a show and tell confession."

The three of us got out of the car and followed Sheriff Tolan into the building. Before long we found ourselves in an interrogation room with the three of us on one side of the desk and the sheriff and Karl on the other side, with the box of evil between us.

Sheriff Tolan spread out his hands. "Well, who would like to start?"

Maude leaned forward. "About two weeks ago, Flora Harstone was struck down with a curse. We are trying to work out how to break it. After hearing about a golem running around the forest we decided to investigate to see if the two situations were linked." Maude pointed to the box. "Inside that box is a curse tablet which we believe is targeting Flora."

"Two weeks. You have been sitting on this situation for two weeks, and nobody thought to notify me that there is a rogue witch in Walker Bay."

Maude drew herself up. "This is coven business. We were not obliged to bring this to the Sheriff's Department."

Tilda and I winced. Even I could see that was precisely the wrong thing to say.

Sheriff Tolan slammed a hand down on the table. "You have recklessly endangered this town. I should lock you up for that alone." He waited for a few moments as if pulling back his anger.

"Who is involved in this?"

I could tell that Maude didn't want to give him any more information, but the sooner the sheriff got what he wanted, the sooner we would get out of here. Hopefully.

"Margot, Isobel, Tilda and I have been researching ways to break the curse. We reached out to the rest of the coven a couple of days ago, hoping to get further information. Unfortunately, our search hasn't been very fruitful. The first real break we had was last night when Sadie came across the golem. We knew it had to be protecting something important, so we went up there to find what it was. That brought us to the curse tablet." She clasped her hands together and gave the sheriff her best grandmother look. "The sooner we can study that tablet, the sooner we can try to work out a way to break it."

"That would be great except I have a dead body on my hands. I'm guessing Helen Napier is involved in this somehow."

Maude shook her head. "We have no knowledge of that. Helen Napier was magically bound due to an attempt to cast a curse twenty years ago. We were simply trying to get information from her in the hopes she would help."

"From what I've heard it would be more likely that Helen would curse Flora, rather than help her," the sheriff mused.

"True, she would be one of our suspects, but her death means there was somebody else involved."

"Do you have any idea who?" Sheriff Tolan asked.

"No, but they put in place a dissipation spell which also destroyed Helen Napier's soul, so if you were planning on asking one of the coven members to try to communicate with her ghost, you're out of luck."

"Great, do you have any suspects yet?"

Maude shook her head. "Our energy for now is focused on breaking the curse. Once that's done, the coven will be looking into who is able to do this." Maude paused. "If you want to know where I think you should look, it would be the Path Coven."

"Do you have any real evidence to back up that statement, or is it just reflex to blame them?"

Maude shrugged. "Not really, I just wouldn't be shocked."

The sheriff leaned back in his chair and watched the group thoughtfully. "I'm starting to get an understanding of what has happened and what everybody's role is." He settled his gaze on me. "Except for you, Miss Goodwin. You're the one part of this puzzle which doesn't quite fit. How did you come to be a part of this situation?"

I had no idea how to answer this one. As I was trying to think up something to say, Maude beat me to it.

"I kidnapped her."

My mouth dropped open. Of all the ways I thought she would play this conversation, the possibility of her going with the truth had not once entered my mind.

"You what?"

"When Flora first went down with the curse, we thought it was a sleeping potion overdose. We wanted to do a healing spell which is strengthened by having someone of the patient's bloodline. We went looking for a member of Flora's family to help us. None of them would even talk to us and I got frustrated. I found Sadie, knocked her out with a stun spell, and brought her back here."

Sheriff Tolan looked shocked. "Are you out of your mind? Her coven is going to go ballistic when they find out about this."

Maude lowered her head. "She has no coven. Until four days ago, Sadie had no idea that she might have witch blood in her. She knew nothing of our world."

"Are you saying you broke the number one law of our people?"

"If you're asking me whether I brought someone into Walker Bay that had no idea of the paranormal world, the answer is yes. But she is a witch, we just haven't had the opportunity to explore her abilities yet." Maude straightened. "We believe Sadie is Flora's niece. The coven is claiming her as a lost soul."

"Lost soul?" I muttered out of the side of my mouth.

"Paranormal who is taken from our world as a child and needs to be rescued," Tilda replied.

"Doesn't quite fit."

"It's close enough," snapped Maude.

I raised an eyebrow and gave her an expression my

mother had perfected when I was a teenager and got a little mouthy.

"I apologize," she amended. "It's been a trying couple of weeks. I shouldn't take it out on you."

"No," Sheriff Tolan interrupted. "Taking out your bad mood on the woman you snatched off the streets is not usually considered good form."

He stood up abruptly. "Iversen, you stay here. Do not let these women move. If they do, you have my permission to use a stun gun on them. Miss Goodwin, you're with me."

That really didn't sound good. I followed the sheriff out of the interrogation room and into the much more pleasant surroundings of his office.

"Take a seat."

Ignoring his gesture towards the chair at his desk, I sat down on a small couch that was at the side of the room. I just got out of an interrogation room. I didn't really feel the need to repeat the experience in a slightly nicer setting.

Realizing that if he sat behind his desk he would be talking to the side of my head, Sheriff Tolan placed himself on the small table in front of the couch.

"Congratulations, Miss Goodwin, you just jumped from perpetrator to victim."

"I am not a victim." I wanted to make that perfectly clear. This was getting us nowhere. We needed to be studying the tablet and helping Flora. "If you're thinking of trying to charge Maude, I'm not going to help you. In fact, I'll be the most difficult witness you've ever had."

"Why does that not surprise me?" He studied me for a few seconds, those pale eyes searching mine. "Have you ever heard of Stockholm Syndrome?"

"You're talking about someone who starts to sympathize and have a relationship with the people who have taken them captive."

The sheriff nodded.

"It doesn't apply here."

Sheriff Tolan looked skeptical. "From where I'm sitting, you're pretty much a textbook example."

We really didn't have time for this. "Look, you're a witness to the fact that I have been able to wander freely. Sure, my initial meeting with these women was unpleasant, and I probably still have issues from the head injuries, but I believe in what they're doing, and I can't turn my back on Flora."

Sheriff Tolan leaned back in his chair. "You realize that this situation puts me in a bad position."

"Sure, let's make it all about you."

The sheriff let out a bark of laughter that sounded rusty. "You know, for someone who has probably had a shocking few days, you're coping amazingly well."

"Don't worry, I have a feeling there is going to be an epic meltdown in my future. I'll try to be very far away from this town when that happens."

"I would appreciate that," he replied, a smile on his face.

I felt a quiver in my stomach that I ruthlessly quashed. Despite the kiss that still filled my thoughts, the last thing I needed was an irrational attraction to the man who turned into a raging monster. I may not have had a lot of romantic luck, but that would be pushing it, even for me.

"My problem is that my legal hold over the coven is tenuous at best. That's what happens when you have more than one legal system people have to live by. This situation is a perfect example of what makes my job so difficult. The first step that the coven should have taken as soon as Flora was cursed would have been to notify me. Instead they kidnapped you and now I'm dealing with at least one rogue witch, a ritual murder, and Flora's attempted murder. Nobody is speaking to me and, because it's coven business, I can't make them talk." He dragged a hand over his face. I could see the stress was taking its toll. "So, Miss Goodwin, how would you suggest I deal with this mess?"

I licked my lips and was surprised at the way his eyes zeroed in on the movement. A flash of heat went through me and I wanted to kick myself. I so did not have the time for this.

"The first thing that we need to do is to break the curse that's holding Flora. Once we do that, I think that the coven will throw everything into finding out who did this. If you show leniency now, I promise I will talk to Maude about having the coven give you complete access to assist with your investigation."

"You really think she'll agree to that?" the sheriff asked doubtfully.

"I will use every bit of guilt that she has over kidnapping me to get them to help you."

"You really believe she has that much guilt?"

I raised an eyebrow. "I should hope so, she knocked me out and stuck me in the trunk of a car for almost twenty-four hours."

The sheriff groaned. "Please stop giving me details. The more you tell me, the harder it is to ignore what they did."

"You don't have a choice. Your only other option is to stick me on the stand and watch your case implode in a spectacular fashion. I can be very creative when I want to be."

"I know that, it's the only reason I'm willing to go along with this."

I stood up abruptly. "Well then, you need to let us go now. I really don't think it's very kind of you to leave Karl in there with Maude."

I walked towards the door but stopped when I felt a hand on my arm. The sheriff cleared his throat. "I need to know if you're going to tell anyone about what you saw."

I hated seeing the vulnerability in his eyes. Since I'd arrived, Sheriff Tolan had been consistent. He'd been annoying as hell, but he'd been consistently annoying. I didn't like what I was seeing here.

"I'm not even sure what I saw last night. I only just found out that my family doctor is a centaur. I'm trying to limit the amount of new information I take in at any one time." I put my hand over his. "Your secret is safe with me. I won't tell anyone."

The sheriff smiled tightly and let go of my arm. "Thank you, I'm not sure what I'm going to do but I'd prefer to make the decision myself."

"Good, now that that's settled, I think we should go rescue Karl. Maude doesn't strike me as the patient type."

"Why'd you think I left him in there?"

"Why did you tell him I was kidnapped?" I asked as we headed back to Flora's house. "He could have locked you up. I'm pretty sure he still wants to lock you up."

"Course he wants to lock her up," Tilda said. "She was one of his teachers in high school. Tell me one person who would pass up that opportunity."

"You're a teacher?" For some reason the thought that my kidnapper was charged with the molding of impressionable young minds was slightly disturbing.

"Retired," Maude said dryly as if she knew exactly what I was thinking.

"Oh, that's good."

"The school district agrees," muttered Tilda from the back seat.

"What the…?" Maude barked as she pulled up at Flora's house. A car I hadn't seen before was parked out the front.

"That's Marigold's car," noted Tilda.

I searched my memories of the last few days as we walked up to the house, trying to remember where I had heard that name before. A familiar figure stepped out onto the porch, the witch healer who had put a salve on the cut on my hand.

"What are you doing here, Marigold?" Maude sounded wary.

Marigold clasped her hands before her and gave the air of a penitent nun. "Isobel and Margot needed someone to watch over Flora while they looked into something."

"Looked into what?"

Marigold shrugged. "I don't know. It just seemed important."

"Sadie," Maude ordered urgently, "check on Flora."

I raced into the house and made my way to the bedroom. A cursory look didn't indicate that anything was wrong, but there was something happening with the blue aura that surrounded the woman on the bed. I put my hand on her arm and, unlike the last few times I had done that, the tendrils barely swept my skin before falling back down.

"What's happening?" I asked Maude who was hurrying through the door.

"She's getting weaker," Maude replied as she took up a position on the opposite side of the bed. She brushed Flora's hair to one side. "I hate this." I could see the sheen of tears in her eyes.

I pulled back my hand. "We're not doing her any good here. We need to look at that tablet."

Maude followed me into the kitchen where we found Tilda at the table alone, staring at the small box which was sitting in front of her.

"Where's Marigold?" Maude asked sharply.

Tilda sighed. "She kind of got the idea that she wasn't very welcome, so she took off."

"I didn't..."

"I know you don't mean to do anything, Grandma, but you need to think before you speak. Marigold is the coven healer and she's a little miffed that she wasn't called in as soon as Flora became…whatever it is that she is. After this is dealt with, I can pretty much guarantee there are going to be issues regarding how we shut the others out. You can't make unilateral decisions like we've done without there being consequences."

Maude lowered her head. "I know, it just took me by surprise that someone else was here."

"Why should it? The coven knows what happened to Flora, we can and should be calling on all of them to help. Margot and Isobel did the right thing getting Marigold to watch Flora."

It was when they were arguing that I could see the similarities between the two women. They had identical eyes that flashed when they were trying to make a point.

"I don't mean to interrupt what I'm sure is a discussion that could go on for days, but I'm pretty sure that we have a limit to how long Flora can hold on," I said, hoping that they didn't decide to turn on me.

"Very well," Maude said. "We need to examine the tablet."

I went to open the box but stopped when Tilda put a hand on my arm.

"Before you open it you should be aware that the box is as important as the tablet. It's blackthorn."

If it was at all possible, Maude drew back a bit further from the box. "Are you sure?"

From the look on her face I could tell that Tilda was not impressed by Maude questioning her expertise. "I'm the one with a forest growing inside my house. If I'm saying it's blackthorn, that's what it is."

I raised a hand. "As the non-witch in the room, what is blackthorn?"

"You are a witch," Maude snapped, "but dealing with that is a problem for another day. Blackthorn is a type of wood that has always been associated with witches. Its use has been outlawed for decades as it does have some less than desirable magical properties." She tapped her chin thoughtfully. "You know, when we first looked around the cave, we didn't see the box. It was only when you pointed it out that it became apparent. It's interesting that we were unable to see it initially, but you could."

"It was in the shadows of the cave, easy to miss."

"Maybe."

"I've never heard of blackthorn making something invisible to a trained witch," interrupted Tilda, "Blackthorn isn't dark magic on its own, but it magnifies and directs dark magic. It's like the diabolical frosting on an evil cupcake."

"So, what happens when you put a curse tablet inside a blackthorn box."

Tilda grimaced. "Kind of like a nuclear missile with an unmissable guidance system."

"Okay, just so I'm completely caught up with everyone else. By having a curse tablet in a blackthorn box, you're saying that things have now got worse."

"So much worse," murmured Maude.

"Let's get this thing out," I said as I opened the box. Using the scarf, I grabbed the tablet and laid it on the table. By now I knew that holding the curse tablet with the scarf was completely useless, kind of like wiping the dirt off a piece of food that has fallen on the floor. Still, it gave me a sense of protection. At this stage, I needed that.

The three of us peered at the tablet, only to find symbols carved into it.

"I thought there would be words," I complained. "How are we supposed to break the curse if there are no words telling us what the curse is about."

"These are ancient symbols of witchcraft. When we start your training, you will learn them." Maude pointed to one symbol which looked like a bird with one leg and an extra wing. "This symbol represents Flora or rather her position as coven leader."

No matter how much I squinted there was no way I would have been able to tell that.

"And this symbol represents chains or keeping her confined."

Nope, I wouldn't have picked that one either. It looked like a spread-eagled spider that had been pinned to a piece of cardboard.

"And this one…"

I put my hand up. "We don't have time for a lesson here. You're going to need to give me the translated version."

Maude sucked in her breath and I could tell she was trying to suppress her natural desire to teach. "Basically, the tablet says that Flora has committed a crime against the witch who created it and her punishment is to be trapped inside her mind, her body unable to move until the time of her natural death."

"That's it?"

Maude nodded sadly. "Most curse tablets are pretty simple. It takes a lot of time and effort to carve stone, so that generally cuts down on the loquaciousness."

"Loquaciousness?"

"Too many words," Tilda supplied as she rolled her eyes. "Grandma was an English teacher. Sometimes she likes to show off."

"I'm guessing smashing the curse tablet won't destroy the curse."

Maude smiled sadly then shocked me by picking up the tablet and throwing it at the ground where it made a solid thud. I picked it up and examined it. Not even one small chip had come off.

"How is that possible?"

"In theory, destroying the tablet should break the curse. In practice, the magic used to create the tablet makes the stone indestructible."

I furrowed my brow. "So, you need to get rid of the dark magic and then destroy the tablet."

"That's the idea," said Maude.

There was a noise at the front of the house, and we all looked up.

"We've found it." Isobel stalked in and slammed a book on the table. Dust flew up from the pages.

"Found what?" asked Maude after she stopped coughing.

Margot was bouncing on her feet with excitement. "Isobel found a way to break the curse."

"Are you sure?" Maude looked skeptical.

"Yes," Isobel replied. "About a hundred years ago a coven was able to break a curse tablet using a cleansing ritual, and they wrote down how they did it."

Maude furrowed her brow. "A cleansing ritual? I wouldn't think that would be powerful enough."

"It requires the whole coven to be involved."

Maude still looked skeptical. "We need to know more."

Isobel took in a breath and I could see she was trying to calm herself. "During the fourteenth century there was a witch hunter called Paul Raynard. He did what most witch hunters did and went after innocent human girls who were falsely accused of witchcraft by jealous neighbors. However, one day he was unfortunate enough to execute a real witch. Her sister created a curse tablet that basically meant that every Raynard male died in his thirtieth year. Those that were older than thirty, including Paul, survived but they watched all the younger males in the family die without fail before their thirtieth birthday, starting with Paul Raynard's beloved younger brother. If any Raynard male tried to destroy the tablet they would die immediately. Paul Raynard met his end doing just that, driven mad by the knowledge he had destroyed his family. By about a hundred years ago they'd gone from a very large family to just one Raynard male left. Michel Raynard was almost thirty and his wife was pregnant. He sought out a local coven leader who claimed he would be able to help the child, but that Michel would die immediately if the attempt was made. Michel Raynard was desperate to save his child, so he accepted what was happening to him and didn't fight the curse, all so his child would be saved if it was a boy. Raynard relinquished the curse tablet to the coven. The whole coven took part in a cleansing ritual. Michel Raynard died that night and his son was born three days later." Isobel smiled. "The child died peacefully in his sleep at the age of seventy-four. The Raynard family has flourished ever since." She started flicking open the pages of the book. "Here, read it yourself."

Maude and Tilda pored over the book, their eyes racing across the page.

Tilda looked up with a smile on her face. "It might work. We've got everything we need. It's a clear night tonight, perfect for a cleansing ritual."

Maude hesitated. "Maybe we should do more research so we can make sure we do it right."

"She's getting weaker," I reminded her. "How much longer do you think she'll last?"

Maude took in a deep breath. "You're right, we need to move on this now. The longer we wait the less chance she'll be able to pull out of it."

Tilda was already moving and grabbing her phone, ready to gather the army of witches.

"We'll need to take the tablet," motioned Margot.

"Keep it separate from the blackthorn box," cautioned Maude. The last thing that monstrosity needs is extra strength."

"So, what do you need me to do?" I asked.

Maude stopped and glanced over at Isobel who shrugged. "We need you to stay here with Flora."

"I thought you required a family member," I pointed out.

"We needed a family member for a healing spell. A cleansing ritual is something completely different. Having an untrained witch will drag down the power level. You can't be anywhere near the coven while we do this."

Well, that felt like a kick in the teeth. After everything I'd been through, I didn't think I'd be tossed over at the end.

Isobel left the room, and Maude came over and put a hand on my shoulder. "I'm sorry, I know you want to be a part of this, but we will need every bit of power that we can get hold of for this to work. The coven will be performing this ritual tonight in the magic circle. It is the place and time that we will have the most power. I need you to stay with Flora and call Tilda if there is any sign that something is going wrong."

"Tilda will be taking a phone into the magic circle during a cleansing ritual?" I wanted to clarify that to ensure I heard it properly.

"She'll have it on vibrate," Maude reassured me.

That didn't make it any less weird.

26

*Y*ou never really notice how quiet a place can be until you've had a day of chaos in it. The afternoon and evening had been spent pulling together every item and person that the coven thought could assist in the cleansing ritual. In what I was informed by a scandalized Tilda was a highly unusual event, the coven didn't limit itself to witches. After the numerous times the account of the cleansing ritual was read, it was determined that other species of paranormals could be brought in to up the power quotient. In that one afternoon I got more of an education in paranormal magic levels than I ever thought possible. The one thing that shone through was that Flora wasn't just important to the coven, she was a pillar of the Walker Bay community, and they were terrified at the thought of a future without her.

"Take care of her and remember to contact us if you see any change." Despite the urgency of the situation, Maude seemed to be reluctant to leave.

"I won't move from her side," I promised.

Maude nodded sharply and glanced over at Flora before hurrying out of the house.

I closed the door behind her and took up my place by Flora's bed, my hand grasping hers. I had never felt more useless in my entire life. For two hours I sat like that, desperately trying to see some change in her condition, but there was nothing. I bent my head over our clasped hands and closed my eyes. I was surprised when I felt a swirling dizziness and then the familiar cold bathing my skin.

"Flora," I breathed. I didn't understand this. Every other time I had come into this cell, I had been asleep. I was as positive as I could be that I hadn't even been close to sleeping this time. I looked around the room, finding Flora with her back against the wall and her head resting against her bent knees. As I stepped closer to her my attention was caught by something which hadn't been there the last time I visited. "What is that doing here?"

Built into the wall of the dungeon was an exact copy of the curse tablet, but this one had thick black tendrils wrapped around it, more dense than the ones on the blackthorn box.

Flora lifted her head and I could see that the effort cost her. "It just appeared, maybe a day ago, maybe more, maybe less. I can't tell anymore."

The same time that we found the tablet in the cave. That could not be a coincidence.

I knelt down beside Flora as she slumped to the ground, and pushed the hair back from her face. "What's going on?"

She licked her lips which had cracked so much they were bleeding. "Ever since that thing appeared, it's like my strength is being sucked out of me. The last hour it has been getting worse."

I paled as I worked out the timing. "The coven is trying to break the curse."

"Curses can't be broken, not even by the whole coven."

"They think they can," I insisted. "We found a spell in some old book that was used by a coven about a hundred years ago to successfully break a curse."

"The Raynard curse," Flora croaked.

"Yes, the coven thinks that now that we've found the curse tablet, if they use that spell as the basis, they can break this curse."

Flora shook her head. "It won't work."

"Why not?"

"It was a hoax. The Raynard curse was never broken."

"How can you say that? The baby was saved from the curse. His father was the last Raynard to die."

"Michel Raynard was not the father of his wife's child. Michel Raynard was the last Raynard to die from that curse because he was the last Raynard. That curse wasn't broken, it died out because there were no more men of the Raynard line."

"Are you sure?" I whispered.

"The coven leader knew because he was the father of Antonia Raynard's child. They'd been having an affair. By claiming the curse was broken by his coven, he gained power and prestige in the eyes of other covens. By never claiming his child, the baby was assumed to be a Raynard and was able to inherit the Raynard fortune." Flora broke off as a fit of coughing overtook her. "Very few people know the truth. That is why the legend still stands."

I slumped to the ground next to Flora. "It won't work."

I could see the defeat in Flora's eyes. It was like all the light had been extinguished. She put her hand over mine. "There isn't anything you can do. My fate was sealed the moment the curse was unleashed."

No, it couldn't end like this. I stood up quickly and strode over to the tablet on the wall. Maybe in here there was something that could be done about it. I glanced back at Flora and felt my resolve grow, there wasn't much I could do that would make this worse. I studied the tablet, all the time fighting the growing nausea I felt being so close to an object of evil. The black tendrils that were wrapped around it seemed to be holding it in place. Without giving much thought to a plan of action, I started pulling at the tendrils. I shuddered at the first contact, it wasn't just the slimy feeling that they had against my skin, it was more that they were leaving bands of darkness up my hands and my arm. I grasped a handful of tendrils and yanked, surprised to see them pull away from the wall in my hand. With a flick of my wrist I tossed it to the opposite corner of the room. Then I pulled on the next one and repeated until the tablet was free of the darkness that was now writhing in a dark mass in the corner, some of the tendrils still trying to reach out to us. Ignoring the darkness, I studied the tablet. It seemed to be wedged into the wall, rather than a part of it. Using the tips of my fingers I tried prying it out and was surprised when it fell into my hands.

I glanced over and found Flora watching me with wide eyes. I sat next to her on the cold ground and placed it at her feet. "What do we do next?" I asked urgently.

"There is nothing that can be done."

I wanted to scream in the face of Flora's resignation. I didn't believe her. There had to be something. Despite knowing the futility of the action, I grabbed the tablet and hurled it at the opposite wall, expecting to hear that dull thud that I'd heard when Maude did the same. Instead, a flash of light filled the room. I ducked my head and covered Flora's, terrified that despite my earlier thoughts, I'd been able to make things worse.

I lifted my head to find myself back in Flora's bedroom. I quickly looked up, terrified at the thought that my reckless anger may have killed her. Instead, I saw her eyes fluttering as if she was waking from a peaceful night's sleep.

"It worked," I breathed as Flora's eyes focused on me. "I'll call the others."

Flora's arm shot out and gripped my hand with a surprising strength. "You can't tell the others what you did," she croaked.

"Why not?"

"Only a cursebreaker could have done what you just did. Cursebreakers are not allowed to live. That edict still stands, even after hundreds of years. If anyone confirms what you are, they'll kill you. Let them believe that the whole coven was needed to break this curse. If we don't, you will never know peace again in your life."

That just seemed really unfair. "I'm not a cursebreaker," I said desperately. "It was just because the tablet appeared within your mind, it must have been a weaker version." I was grasping at straws, I had no idea what had just happened.

Flora gave me a grim smile. "What do you think I was trying to do all day before you showed up. You don't think that I tried to destroy that tablet from the moment it appeared." She caught my chin and forced me to look into her eyes. "I've been the coven leader of Walker Bay since I was thirteen years old, and I'm the strongest witch you are ever likely to meet. I couldn't get near that thing, but you were able to tear away the dark magic and destroy it. Nobody but a cursebreaker could do that."

"What are we going to do?" I asked, the realization and fear beginning to build in me.

Flora pulled herself up in the bed. "We let the coven believe that they managed to break the curse. That way nobody will even think to look in your direction."

"So, we provide history with another hoax," I murmured.

"It's the only way."

"I better contact them anyway. I was told to call Tilda if anything changed."

"I hate that Tilda brings that phone of hers into the magic circle. There is just something so wrong about that," Flora grumbled.

Despite the circumstances I smiled. It was both surreal and comforting to hear her complain about new-fangled technology taking over the world as she struggled out of the bed. I held out my arm to help give her leverage and she gripped it as she tried to stand.

"Who found the spell breaking the Raynard curse?" she asked.

"Isobel."

Flora stopped still. "That's not possible."

"She found it in one of the old coven books that are stored in the back room of the library. We've been poring over those for days and it was the only thing we found."

"No, I mean it's not possible because Isobel is one of the people who know that it was a hoax."

"Then why would she...?" The answer hit me. "You're not thinking that Isobel did this to you. She's your friend. Why would she put a curse on you?"

A chilling voice came from the doorway. "Because we need new leadership."

27

*T*his was not the way things were supposed to happen.

"I don't understand," I said as I warily watched one of the women I had trusted make her way across the room. "Why would you do this?"

"We need Flora out of the way," Isobel said simply. "We need a leader who isn't so willing to bend to every whim of the Conclave."

The worst part was there was no emotion behind that statement. I would have expected hate or anger, but there was nothing.

Flora drew herself up as straight as she could, but I could still feel her weight against me. "And who did you have in mind to replace me?"

Isobel smiled. "Why, me of course, there really isn't a better candidate."

My mouth dropped open. "You cursed Flora and I'm assuming you were the one who murdered Helen Napier. How does that make you the better choice?"

Isobel waved her hand in the air. "We needed Flora out of

the way, and Helen was useful but unstable. She may have caused problems later on."

"So, you decided to kill her and destroy her soul."

Isobel shrugged with a nonchalance which terrified me. "Revolutions are rarely bloodless. Anyone who says otherwise is lying."

"Is that what this is?" wheezed Flora. "A revolution?"

"Can't you see it? Witchcraft has always been about people being free to practice any way they wish, to expand their knowledge, but these days we're drowning in rules and bindings. The Conclave is destroying our culture and our heritage, for what? So, we can play nice with the other paranormals, or is there a plan to introduce us to the humans and make us more palatable for them?" She straightened, her eyes flashing. "Do you know how many books I have had to save from being destroyed on the orders of the Conclave."

"You saved them?" Flora's voice was horrified.

Isobel smiled grimly. "How do you think I became so adept at curses?"

"They were under destruction orders because they are so dangerous."

"And yet, so useful. Do you have any idea how it feels to craft a golem? To create life with your own two hands." Isobel looked down at her hands as if she could still see the clay, but then she frowned. "Although the fact that the curse broke must mean there was something wrong with it. Maybe there was a built-in time limit."

Sure, I was happy to go with that explanation.

"What you're doing is wrong," Flora said, her voice wavering. "How can you not see that? How is Margot going to cope with this? You can't tell me that she agrees with you."

I'd forgotten about Margot who, until ten minutes ago, I would have bet money was the evil twin.

For the first time I thought I saw a flash of remorse.

"Margot will understand what we're trying to do here once she has seen the vision."

"What are you going to do?" I asked as I strained to hold Flora up.

"The coven will be returning soon. They are going to find that the curse was unable to be broken and that it has expanded to claim Flora's niece."

I looked down at Flora who was listing to the side. Running was not an option.

"You won't have time," I said desperately. "The coven will be here soon. They'll know what you've done."

There was a time not too long ago when I would have been comforted by Isobel's smile. That time was long gone.

"I started preparing for this moment the day you arrived." She held out a new curse tablet and placed it on the ground in front of her. "When I discovered you were able to pull your niece into your mind, Flora, I knew the original curse needed to be strengthened, so this will serve to remove both of you." She pulled out a knife, held it above her head and started chanting.

I put my arm around Flora and slowly lowered her to the ground. "Run if you can," I whispered urgently, although I knew it would be impossible.

I turned and watched as Isobel cut her hand and a single drop fell to the tablet. In that moment of distraction, I rushed towards her, only to be stopped by a flash of light blinding me. I groaned and covered my eyes as I sank to the floor, expecting any moment to find myself back in that cell, except this time having no way out. Ten seconds passed and I didn't feel that bitter cold that had become so familiar. I looked up and blinked to clear the flashing black spots that bounced around in front of me. Isobel was slumped on the ground, blood oozing from the wound on her hand onto the curse tablet.

"What happened?" I croaked as I looked over at Flora who was in the same position I was in.

"She tried to cast a curse on a cursebreaker. It must have rebounded on her."

"You mean she..."

Flora nodded, a grim expression on her face. "She's now trapped in her body, exactly like I was."

"Why didn't it work on you this time?"

Flora smiled. "When you tried to rush her, you stepped in front of me. The curse hit you first and bounced back at her as if you were a shield. It didn't get anywhere near me."

"I could go in and break the curse," I said reluctantly. I know that a good person is supposed to be all about forgiveness but, considering the woman was planning to trap me in my own body for all eternity, I was finding it hard to be that enlightened. Nevertheless, sometimes you say things, not because you want to, but because it's expected.

Flora shook her head. "No, Isobel chose her fate the first time she ventured into using dark magic. If you break the curse, she will know what you are. She will use that information to turn you or to destroy you. Neither of those options are acceptable."

That brought us to a conversation I wasn't sure I wanted to have. "According to Isobel you're all about the rules of the Conclave." I swallowed nervously. "I'm pretty sure harboring a cursebreaker goes against all those rules."

"Family comes first," she said simply. "If you plan to stay in Walker Bay, I would suggest you becoming my apprentice. Between us, we could see how far your power goes and how much it can be controlled."

"I don't know," I said as I knelt down beside Flora and helped her up. "I'm not sure if I'm ready for this world." And I really didn't know if I was ready for the emotion that swept through me at Flora's claiming me as family.

Flora patted my cheek. "I hope you are, because I have a very bad feeling that this is not ending with Isobel. I could use some help."

"What are we going to do about her?" I asked, my gaze directed at the figure lying on the floor.

Flora sighed and I could see tears in her eyes. "For many years she was a good friend. I don't know why she took the path she did, but I can't forget those years. We will make her as comfortable as possible until we can find a way to get her out of the hell she's in without exposing you."

First of all, there was something else we needed to do. "I'm going to call the sheriff."

Flora raised an eyebrow. I recognized that stubborn look, I'd seen it in the mirror on more than one occasion. "This is coven business."

I shook my head. "Not anymore it isn't. She murdered Helen Napier and she tried to kill you. If she isn't the only rogue witch gunning for you, we're going to need as much help as we can get. This could spread and put the town at risk." I looked her directly in the eyes. "I'm not asking permission. He needs to know what happened."

I could see Flora wasn't happy with my decision, but I'd made a deal with Sheriff Tolan and I wasn't going to back out of it.

When he arrived with paramedics in tow, I could see that he wasn't any happier with the situation than Flora was. His gaze locked with Flora's as she sat in her bed. The paramedics rushed over to Isobel, firing questions at us. Flora answered their questions calmly and succinctly, completely in charge of the situation despite her weakened state.

Sheriff Tolan pulled me into the kitchen while Isobel was being worked on. "I need you to explain what happened here."

With great care I outlined the version of the night's

events that Flora and I had decided was suitable for public consumption. It was as close to the truth as we could possibly get without implicating the innocent, namely me. From the look on his face I didn't think he was buying it.

"Are you sure that's everything?" he asked with skepticism in his voice.

"I'm telling you everything that I understand." That was the truth. There were so many things about tonight that were beyond my comprehension, but one thing stood out. If anyone found out the truth about how the curse had been broken, according to some ancient law that hadn't been used in three hundred years, my life was forfeit. Despite the fact that Sheriff Tolan wasn't beholden to witch law, I still wasn't sure if I trusted him with that little piece of information.

"I'm having trouble believing…"

Fortunately, the rest of that accusation was interrupted by the arrival of Maude, Tilda and Margot. My stomach clenched as I realized what Margot was about to face.

"What's happening?" gasped Maude. "Why is there an ambulance here? Did something happen to Flora?"

Sheriff Tolan raised both his hands. "Flora is fine, the curse seems to be broken." He glanced at me meaningfully. "Miss Goodwin is going to explain things to you out here." He looked over at Margot and his expression gentled. "Miss Fulton, there has been an incident with your sister. I need you to follow me and I'll take you through what happened."

Margot's hand flew to her mouth and, despite my expectation that she would demand explanations immediately, she meekly followed the sheriff into Flora's bedroom where I heard her cry out before hearing Flora's soothing murmurs.

"What happened?" demanded Maude.

I waved a hand to the chairs around the kitchen table. "Grab a seat, this could take a while." When we were all seated, I broke the news to them as gently as I could. "Isobel cast the curse."

"No," Maude said calmly. "I don't know why you think that but it's untrue."

I knew this was going to be a shock to the two women. "She admitted it. She believes the Conclave is destroying witch culture, and that Flora is a puppet of the Conclave and needs to be replaced."

Maude shook her head adamantly, her voice rising in anger. "I don't know why you're doing this but I'm not going to believe it until Isobel tells me herself."

"She won't be able to do that," I sighed. "She tried to cast another curse and it backfired. She's now in the position that she put Flora in."

As if to prove my point, the paramedics started wheeling Isobel out with Margot following, softly weeping as she was held up by Sheriff Tolan.

Maude jumped up. "I'm going with them," she insisted as she elbowed the sheriff out of the way. I didn't miss the furious look she cast at me as they walked out.

"Did Flora explain?" I asked.

Sheriff Tolan nodded. "She's not going to have an easy time of it. She doesn't seem to have had a clue what Isobel was doing."

"But Flora is okay? The curse was broken." Tilda's eyes were red, and I could see she was struggling with what was happening.

I put my hand over hers and she gripped it hard, as if trying to find an anchor. "Flora seems fine, but she is still very weak. The curse may have been broken but she is vulnerable and needs protection."

Tilda wiped her eyes with her sleeve. "You're right, I'll get onto that straight away. We need the doctor here to check her out."

She pulled out a phone and started organizing as if her heart hadn't just been broken. I had to admit that I was very impressed.

Sheriff Tolan stepped up next to me and lowered his voice. "I've got to get going now and see what I can find out from Isobel's house." He ducked his head and those pale eyes caught mine. "There are going to be numerous investigations into this. Not only my department but the Conclave is going to want to get in on this as well. By the end of this nobody is going to have any secrets."

I swallowed nervously. That sounded bad. Really, really bad.

*D*espite my firm belief that there was no chance I would be able to sleep, I woke up refreshed and forever grateful that I did not end up back in that cell explaining to Isobel why her curse had failed so spectacularly. After the paramedics and Sheriff Tolan had left, Tilda and I had organized a medical examination of Flora and someone to care for her for the next several weeks, which is how long Doctor Collias believed it would take before Flora was fully recovered. By the time we got back to Tilda's house it was the early hours of the morning, and I'd fallen asleep the second my head hit the pillow. Only a few hours later, in what seemed to be a habit I wanted desperately to break, I found myself wide awake and heading down to the bay. Since coming to this town, I seemed to need this early morning ritual to give me a form of peace, and to deal with the surreal situation I had found myself in. As I sat on the bench, I let myself absorb the peace of the quiet morning and feel rejuvenated to face the day again.

"I thought I'd find you here."

"You know, I would have liked one morning when I

wasn't interrupted while enjoying the sunrise," I grumbled as Maude took a seat next to me.

"I'm sure you'd get one if you decided to stay."

I looked back out over the bay. "I'm not sure yet. This has all happened so fast. I just want to take a step back before making such a leap and throwing away the life I have."

Maude snorted. "You forget, Margot and I watched you before we brought you here. We saw you spend your day at work and your evenings at home. Your coworkers would go out, but you never joined them. You seemed to deliberately keep yourself apart from people."

"What are you talking about? You're making it sound as if I was some crazy cat lady with no social life."

"Let's be honest. Socially speaking, crazy cat lady would have been a step up for you." She smiled sadly at me. "And the worst part is that you were kidnapped almost a week ago and nobody has reported you missing yet."

"Nobody?"

Maude shook her head. "I checked before I came out here." She put her hand gently over mine. "I know you lost your mother recently and grief has a way of messing with you, but you've locked yourself away. I'm betting that isn't what she would have wanted for you."

"It isn't," I agreed, remembering the way my mother loved life. "But I don't know whether she would have wanted me involved in this world either."

Maude settled back on the bench. "Look at it as an adventure." She paused as if contemplating what to say next. "I'm sorry I was angry with you last night."

"I understand," I murmured.

"No, I couldn't believe that Isobel would betray us like that, and I didn't believe you. I shouldn't have done that. I spent a long time speaking to Flora. We need to work out what happened. Isobel was the best of us. For her to turn like that has to serve as a wakeup call."

"Do you really think there could be others?"

"I'm sure there is. If Isobel could be turned, anybody could be."

I tipped my head back and enjoyed the slight breeze on my face. "If I was to stay, I'd need a job."

"Then you're lucky that an opening just came up in the coven library."

I grimaced. I understood gallows humor, but I would think that was a bit too soon.

Maude obviously caught my look. "That wasn't an appropriate way to put it, but we are going to need a replacement for Isobel. If she has been hoarding books on dark magic, we need to find them fast, before someone else does. The library has been her domain for the last few decades. The coven needs to know what has been going on, especially as the Conclave will want answers.

I nodded in understanding. I had to admit that despite the circumstances, the opportunity to take control of the coven library was one that tempted me in a way that nothing had in what seemed like a very long time. Maude was right. Since my mother died, I had been pulling further away from life. Maybe this was a chance for me to rejoin the rest of the world.

"So, are you coming back?"

I looked out over the bay and knew that I felt a kind of peace that I had never felt before. "Yeah, I'll be returning once I've packed up everything back home. It shouldn't take long."

"That's good. After talking to Flora, I spent the rest of the night doing some more research on that curse that trapped her." Maude paused but she kept her eyes out on the bay. "To work as well as it did on a coven leader, it would have required a family member to have a hand in it."

I glanced sharply at Maude. "Does she know?"

"I haven't told her yet, but she's going to find out soon. Even though she hasn't had any family for most of her life, the knowledge that one or more of them deliberately cursed her is going to hurt badly." Maude paused and I could feel her eyes appraising me. "You're going to become very important to her."

"Is that something you've seen in the tea leaves, or are you hoping?"

"A bit of both."

"In that case, I need to get home and start packing." I glanced over at Maude who was trying to hide a small smile. "And since you ladies kidnapped me without stopping to grab my purse, I have no identification. That means I can't get on a plane. One of you is going to be driving me home for the next twenty-four hours."

"I'm sure Tilda will be fine with that."

I grinned. "That hardly seems fair considering she's the one who had no part in the kidnapping."

"It won't be the first time she had to clean up one of my messes," Maude said.

"And I'm sure it won't be the last," I murmured.

Maude's expression sobered. "Your future was always destined to be here, Sadie. I knew that from the first moment I saw you."

I looked back out at the bay that had so quickly become the one place in this world that I found peace, and I had a feeling that she was right.

ABOUT THE AUTHOR

Leonie Gant started her writing career at the age of ten when she stuffed notes in her pencil case full of ideas for mysteries that Nancy Drew and the Hardy Boys should really have been solving. After years of watching mysteries play out in her head she decided that writing them down was the best way to deal with them.

In her life away from writing, she is a voracious reader with not nearly enough time to make her way through all the books she wants to read. She also enjoys bushwalking, sewing and chocolate, possibly not in that order.

To find out more about Leonie Gant and her books

www.leoniegant.com